SEDUCING THE SERPENT

THE FAEVERSE CHRONICLES

HUNTER J SKYE

This is a work of fiction. Names, characters, places, and incidents are either the product of the author's imagination or are used fictitiously, and any resemblance to actual persons living or dead, business establishments, events, or locales, is entirely coincidental.

Seducing the Serpent

Print ISBN: 979-8-9868511-3-6

Contact Information: hunter.j.skye@gmail.com

Cover Art by *Hunter J. Skye*

Visit us at: www.hunterskye.com

Published in the United States of America

For all the daddies out there, you know who you are.

1

LILITH NIGHTKIN

"NIGHT MONSTER"

Domain: Corporis (corporeal)
Kingdom: Fae (children of Adam's first wife)
Phylum: Eros (life)
Class: Khaos (chaos)
Order: Carnem (flesh)
Family: Liliths (succubi)
Genus: Venereae (erotic)
Species: Don't Ask. Not Kidding. Don't.

Not many humans know about our breeding program, and none have been inside an Underhill. If you zip your lip and just listen, I'll tell you the whole bloody story. But remember, I'm Venereae. So, if you don't like sex—get out. *Now.*

I dialed the lights down to zero in the Copulation Room and tried my darndest to ignore the deliciously wet slap of quivering flesh.

"Thank you." The breathy words whispered through the speaker next to the observation window in front of me.

Long, languid moans and quick, staggered panting followed.

Darkness was the only privacy I could give my friend and her specimen.

Watching a respected colleague suck the bark off a rare male dryad with a trunk the size of my forearm took restraint. Buckets of restraint considering I am a Lilith fae in the Phylum Eros and to make things worse, I'm Genus Venereae—a literal sex fairy.

Some think that makes me one of the biggest harlots of the Fae Kingdom, maybe even the whole Corporis Domain. Sure, I like sex. Okay, it's pretty much my raison d'etre, but there are other Eros fae that get way more action than me. *Way more.*

Actually, I'm pretty lonely. And I hang out with humans way too much. In fact, if I'm being honest…I wish I was human. Humans don't have to live underground and follow orders from a bloodythirsty cult of Old World fae. Humans get to choose who they mate with. Humans have ice cream, roller-coasters, and date nights.

I hate you guys. I love you, hate you. Okay, I don't hate you at all, but quit thinking fae are so glamorous and mysterious. I know you've only known about us for twenty years, but we are monsters. Flesh-flaying, soul-sapping, fuck-you-and-kill-you creatures of nightmares. Okay? *Now, shut up.*

Daphne was made of barely room-temperature, living wood, but I'm pretty sure any fae hot or cold-blooded would squirm with desire over that display. Because I'm a Lilith—

more squirming. I can't help it. I'm built for carnal knowledge. The more my friend, Daphne, "knowledged" that giant redwood of a man, the harder I fought not to join in and kick the party up a notch.

Because I know you want to ask, but your lips are zipped, I'll go ahead and confirm two things you may have already heard about Liliths.

First, *yes*, we are all named Lilith and we are all female. *No*, I don't know why. It has to do with our mother, Adam's first wife before Eve. The common belief is the Night Mother made us in her image so completely that we can't even be called by anything else but her name—even Liliths like me who've only been walking the earth for twenty-eight and a half years.

Second, *yes*, we are wanton, and I can confirm that our venereae nature does mean our genitals are a little different than your average hardware.

No, I won't show you.

So, suffice to say, I would have gladly stepped in for my friend. Daphne wasn't a normal breeder. Hell, she wasn't even on the list of restorable bloodlines.

She usually stood on my side of the glass window, taking notes and ensuring copulation. As head of Phylogenetic Recombination, Daphne normally collected a sample of the pre-copulation baby batter with a pipette and vial. This time, she'd licked it off the tight, purple head of her specimen's cock. That image had seared into my mind like a bubbling steak.

Daphne also had the very important job of keeping the official record on all the fae genetic samples I brought in. She didn't usually do the "wet work" as we say. But I'll be damned if she wasn't good at it.

"Turn down the pheromones too, Lil." Daphne's voice crackled through the speaker.

Our underground lab was set up in the outer edge of the Maryland Underhill so that we could utilize things like electricity and be closer to our human counterparts just above us in Hans Jodkins University's Center for Functional Anatomy and Evolution.

The Underhill didn't like it. The Underhill preferred raw energy only, but we couldn't run our computers and com systems on stored lightning bolts.

After a few "conversations" with the Council—the afore mentioned cult of bloodthirsty Old World fae—our comfy little Locus Geographia had relented and allowed the IT Techs to run cable for our facility. But it reserved the right to muck with links and signal strengths whenever something displeased it.

The speaker crackled and squelched.

The observation deck lighting flickered angrily.

Oh yeah, the Underhill was less than pleased about the current activities inside the Copulation Room.

No matter how much Daphne argued the fact, we all knew that the Underhill was sweet on her. Underhills loved trees. Throughout history, every Locus Geographia worth its dirt has crowned itself with one pampered, albeit imprisoned, magnificent tree.

Daphne's pure-blooded status in the Family Arbores, Genus Dryadinae meant she could transform into complete tree form at will. She didn't—probably because she knew it might be considered flirting, and who wanted to arouse a gigantic underground mountain?

Not this girl.

Nevertheless, finding a new community of arboreal fae in the Great Dismal Swamp of Coastal Virginia had been a genetic boon for our program. Until last week, Dr. Daphne Willowine had been the only North American dryad on register.

Finding the lithe blonde non-vegetative dates wasn't a problem. Daphne's classical beauty and legs for days drew plenty of attention. Any fae from any phylum, class, or order would be happy to have her. Hell, she'd even dated a few humans.

Lucky. I hate her too. Not really. Just jealous.

But finding Daphne quality breeding stock was another thing entirely. A fact that sat well with her since she was married to her job and didn't relish the idea of being on the menu.

Regardless, we all had to submit our genetic codes. Like it or not, when an appropriate mate came along, we had to take one for the team like anyone else.

Mmm, the team. The whole team touching me, grabbing me, licking, biting.

Stop!

This is not the time or place to Lilith-out.

Sorry. Where was I?

Unless we found a specimen in the Eros Phylum with enough sexual mana to mate with a Lilith—other than that Ignus Order prick, Hamus—I wasn't getting action anytime soon. Hamus was the hottest of the Fire Fae. Pun intended. An Old Order progenitor and strong enough to mate with anyone. Even me. But Hamus—I actually did hate.

Besides, breeding Liliths required a serious investment in time. Getting around our birthing curse wasn't worth it.

Just ask my mom. Oh wait, we can't. The curse killed her.

"Dialing down," I answered.

A deep and very male groan vibrated through the crackling speaker. The lusty weight in his tone made it clear he had surrendered to the process.

I dialed the pheromones in the aeration system back a little. No need to drive the guy crazy.

We'd already ripped him from his home and what

appeared to be a pretty serious relationship to bring him here and fuck his brains out. I could cut him a little slack.

Daphne didn't need any help in the seduction department anyway.

With any luck, and as long as she didn't open her mouth and over-analyze things, the good doctor could take the coveted, fully paid maternity leave and start enjoying some of her benefits package.

Speaking of packages, I was dying to crank the lights up just a smidge. Not enough for them to notice, just enough so that I could transform to my owl form and use my night vision to get a look at that tree's trunk again. I'd heard dryad males had erections as hard as petrified wood and, from what I could hear—Daphne was enjoying every crystalized inch of his.

I'd closed the door to the Copulation Room tightly, but I could still smell the lust.

Their salty sweat.

His musky woodland animal scent.

Her slick strawberry sweet juices.

I tried to remain professional, but parts south of my navel clenched.

How does Daphne do this job week in and week out?

This was definitely not the position for me.

There are other, more sedate fae in the Eros Phylum, but I'm Khaos Class which means I feed off of desire.

Yes, the succubus stories from the ancient human scrolls are true. But in my fore-mothers' defense—if those young men didn't want the ride of their short lives, they shouldn't have left their bedroom windows open at night. They'd been warned.

The old Liliths had been thicker on the ground in Talmudic times and way more murdery, but the world has changed. Sex with a Lilith is still dangerous, but not always lethal.

I'm pretty sure.

Mostly sure.

Sure enough.

My skin tingled, then itched.

I checked my reflection in the lab's darkened window.

My glamour warped into a paper-thin sheen of rainbows as my human features faded.

The whites of my eyes darkened to black sclera, and my blue irises grayed to a metallic silver. My pink skin drained to a pale blue pallor, and my hair uncoiled from the bouncing brown waves of a healthy female human to the light-drinking onyx of my flat fae locks.

I was in the Underhill, but I was still on duty, so the glamour had to stay in place.

I tugged at the rainbows until they settled over my skin again.

"Coffee break," I announced and thought of the exit that led to the human women's restroom in building D, the Fauna and Flora lab.

As per usual, the Underhill read my thought and shifted to provide a direct path up to the University.

What appeared before me was so jagged and inhospitable, I'd sooner have stepped into a dragon's mouth.

Sharpened protrusions of slick, gray stone sprouted from the floor and ceiling of the tunnel. The only light came from a handful of measly moth pixies who wobbled through the air on their last breaths.

I reached into the darkened maw and plucked one of the fluttering bodies from the air.

Its wing fell off.

Yuck.

Stale pixie.

I couldn't eat that. Moving from the Fae Kingdom to the Human Kingdom required calories. Big, fat kilocalories. It was the Underhill's duty to provide sustenance before one of its denizens passed through an aperture. What the ornery Locus Geographia had just shunted in for me could barely be considered food.

"Did you use the oldest vent possible?" I licked the pixie's remaining wing. My tongue coated with dust. "There's cobwebs on this one."

Pixies were supposed to taste good. According to their color and markings, these bugs should have tasted like the fae equivalent of powdered donuts. Instead, I used my finger to scrape the old wall flavor from my tongue.

I tossed the elderly pixie back into the tunnel.

"What's the problem?" I stared at the empty maw in front of me. "I'm not the one that ordered that." I pointed to the window of the Copulation Room. "If you don't like it, take it up with the Council."

With a sledgehammer crack, the ceiling split above me.

Something heavy rang my skull like a bell.

2

DOMOV THE CLEAN

"THRESHOLD FAE, FAE-IN-THRALL"

Domain: Corporis-transient
Kingdom: Fae
Phylum: Eros
Class: Ordo
Order: Homunculus (little man)
Family: Apercula (those who open)
Genus: Intervallum (space between)
Species: Seriously. Quit asking.

Dust rained into my hair as I stared at the jagged chunk of rock at my feet.

"What the hells?"

The ceiling rumbled above me, threatening to split open again and eject another rock presumably big enough to completely realign my thoughts.

You should know the Underhill doesn't particularly like me but, believe me, that was just plain rude, even in fae culture. And painful.

I rubbed the bump rising on my scalp. It wasn't just Daphne's situation bringing out the worst in our not-so-friendly Locus Geographia. The Underhill had been grumpy for weeks.

"I'm sorry for saying the C-word," I growled. No one wanted to speak to the Council, not even a prehistoric entity like the Underhill.

The Council was made up of the Old Order. Speaking of them even generally could conjure them. The council members were not fae-in-thrall, so they couldn't be summoned, but speaking their names was the same as calling them.

The Underhill ground its stone for a moment as if masticating my apology. Slowly, the serrated floor flattened out and the ceiling smoothed.

A fat, caramel-colored pixie with floppy wings appeared just inside the hallway. I snatched it before it could float away. It gave a satisfying screech as I popped it in my mouth.

Mmm. Butterscotch.

I sucked on it and rolled it on my tongue.

"Thank you." I gave the wall a calming pat, but there was no love lost between us. If I could do this job and live somewhere else, I would.

The passage brightened as I walked along the inclined path through the dense igneous rock that had helped form our host during its volcanic birth so long ago.

I brushed my fingers along the coarse grain of the dark stone walls.

It soon gave way to sparkly metamorphic marble and sandstone quartz.

Milky veins of schist and flecks of flashing mica danced along the walls as I approached the threshold. The Underhill's schist hid semi-precious treasures.

So far, Daphne was the only fae to have stumbled upon them.

I had a feeling, one day, a ring made of rare, raw minerals would drop out of a ceiling and land at her feet. I wondered what stone a mountain would pick to woo a dryad. Would it be a diamond from deep in its heart, or would the Underhill pick something unexpected like calcite or tourmaline? Or would Daphne be offered a giant hunk of blood red jasper? Does she like jasper? What would she say to an offer like that? How do you let a mountain down gently?

The walkway opened into a small, rough-hewn chamber dominated by a vertical pool of shivering light. The opalescent swirl chewed and ground at the computer cables trailing from its mouth. The pulverized rock hissed like sand on a beach. The glimmering detritus thinned in the middle to a skim so fine I could almost see through it.

A lemony hint of human cleaning products drifted through the gateway. It gave the impression that our world and the human realm were the same. But they weren't.

The same planet? Yes.

The same dimension? No.

There were untold fathoms of space between those swirling particles, and I wasn't stupid enough to try and navigate through them alone.

Lucky for me, my favorite threshold fae was on-duty.

"Hey, Domov. When did you get back from Russia?" I waved at the tiny, tiny man who sat in the tiny, tiny chair next to the glittering aperture.

He seemed to love it when I used human geographical names.

Fae had been a part of this planet much longer than humans. Long enough to have named every rock, stream, and continent in the old tongue.

Many of the Old Order refused to learn the utterances of

mortal creatures or the words they'd assigned things, but Domov loved linguistics and hoarded knowledge.

Long, strawberry blond hair covered his three-foot form head to toe.

Recently, it had begun to streak with silver. I liked the mix of gray. It gave him a wizened look, but I'd never say as much.

Threshold Fae were some of the oldest terrestrial beings and easily affected by speech.

Depending on the genus and species, to comment on their appearance in any way could be disastrous. Many an offended guardian had left their posts at the Underhill's various apertures due to an off-hand comment. They were not the kind of guys to give two-week's notice. And they sure weren't the type to return once they'd dropped the F-bomb and stormed.

No threshold fae meant no movement between our realm and any other.

"I was gone less than a fortnight. I'm surprised you noticed my absence," the little man offered modestly.

His voice rumbled out from his homunculus body in a low bass. His age tugged at me like a neutron star. My bones creaked in his gravity.

"It's never the same when you're gone," I complimented.

Orderliness and routine were a threshold faerie's source of pride. The other threshold fae were competent and quick, but nowhere near as friendly.

"How is your *dedushka*?" I inquired politely.

"Grandfather is well-treated, but he is of the old ways. He refuses to move from the henhouse to the main dwelling. The winters are hard on him."

"He's lucky to have a grandson who cares."

The small man's eyes sparkled as I presented him with an

offering. I knew Domov would open the door for me without one, but tradition is nice.

He rolled the clove cigarette in his fingers and sniffed its length.

"No preservatives." He smiled. Then he stood and unbuttoned the seam of the world for me.

I waited a moment to make sure the human restroom on the other side was empty—I didn't like to startle people—and then I stepped through.

My heels clicked on the polished tile. I straightened my staghorn cable knit sweater dress and took a few deep breaths of the thinner air.

The cloying scent of liquid hand-soap burned the artificial lemon smell of the cleaner from my nose. My head buzzed with the unnatural bend of electricity through the walls. Without the Underhill to filter its effects for me, I had to manage the frantic energy on my own.

I walked to the sink and splashed a bit of cold water on my face.

The squirming electrons of the faucet's metal handles vibrated uncomfortably in my hands. I checked my glamour in the mirror. Shadows smudged beneath my human blue eyes. My dark hair hung lank around my shoulders. Not even my glamour could hide my weary state.

No one had missed the irony of a Lilith working in a breeding program, particularly me. Not only could I not take lovers unless I wanted to gamble with their lives, it was also next to impossible for me to reproduce because of the ancient curse on my kind.

I can tell you're curious about the curse. Are you sure you want to know? Curses this old are volatile. Just talking about them could affect your safety.

Okay. I'll give you just the basics. If I want to keep a

child of my own flesh, the spell compels me to first slaughter one hundred of my previous offspring.

That's right. I get to keep kid number one hundred and one. Infanticide is not my thing, and that many births would wear down even my stronger than average fae body. Plus, I'm pretty sure nobody would allow a Lilith to adopt—so, no kids for me. I like kids. Kids are great.

Sometimes I hate being fae.

But as fae employment goes—my job is better than the normal gig. Except for a little quarterly paperwork, my task was primarily to bag and tag genetic specimens.

If you ask me, field agents have the easy part.

Most of the boring office work is performed by Dr. Daphne Willowine, the Director of Phylogenetics, Hennig Dreadmare, our Biomechanics Lab Tech, and Gillian Hobglen, the program's foremost Morphology Research Librarian.

As long as we did our jobs and helped to preserve and promote the restoration of the ancient fae bloodlines, the Council was happy. If the Council was happy, no one died.

I followed the acrid aroma of coffee and hand sanitizer past the Fauna Labs to the break room at the end of the hall. I tapped my fingers against the long, glass Mustelid enclosure as I went, which drew a nasty look from the graduate student on duty. I couldn't help it. The ferrets were so cute.

They vanished beneath the cedar chips at the bottom of their enclosure. I'm sure they could feel my owl form just below the surface of my natural skin, lurking deep beneath my glamour. To them I was probably a horrifying creature just waiting to pounce and eat them for a late dinner.

They were only half wrong.

Underneath my curvy, manicured facade, I was a giant feathered monster with talons as long as their bodies. At least, after sunset. If I chose to shift.

Night Mother, bless them. I would never harm a single silky fur on their tiny, elongated heads, but it was fun to watch them scatter.

The break room was empty, which suited me just fine.

The only human I really liked to be around was Daniel and he was on assignment in Wyoming digging up fossilized treasures from the Eocene Period.

I missed him, but it was just as well that I not see him now. Some nameless emotion wrestled in my stomach like poorly chewed pixies. I hadn't felt this out of control of my Lilith eros since college.

At least back then, I'd had an excuse. The university had been a buffet of lonely, young, unattached men at the peak of their sex drive. And a fair number of sexually curious females as well. Any chaos fae would have been tempted. Luckily, I had been the only Eros on campus and, even though I'm still embarrassed to admit it, the use of restraining charms had saved a few lives.

I bypassed the coffee pots and Styrofoam cups and selected a tea bag and a glass mug. I'd just poured the hot water into my mug when the smell of freshly turned soil spilled into the quiet room.

"Save some for me," Daniel's voice rasped.

3

HAMUS FLAMESIRE

"FATHER OF A MULTITUDE, FIRE DEMON"

Domain: Corporis (corporeal)
Kingdom: Fae
Phylum: Thantos (death)
Class: Ordo (order)
Order: Ignis (fire)
Family: Daemons (demons)
Genus: Draco (dragon)
Species: Literally, none of your business.

A sweet elixir of excitement and embarrassment shot through me. I loved it when Daniel spent too much time outside and the elements swelled his vocal cords. The strong, masculine rumble matched his chiseled arms and rock cliff shoulders.

The sun had lightened the top layer of his loose chocolate curls to the shade of a dusty dirt road. The high plains breezes had filled his locks with the sweet scent of cold mountain streams and warm, waving grasslands.

Daniel's eyes sparkled with that startling aqua of sulfuric geysers. Maybe he had a hint of elemental in him after all. Or maybe that was just my wishful thinking. If Daniel had even a drop of fae blood, I would have claimed him as my calloused, stubble-chinned flesh toy long ago.

My delicious, six-foot two human crush wore the faded 1970s rock band tee-shirt he loved to dig in, but it had shrunk or his muscles had swelled. Either way, his biceps bulged like boulders beneath the whisper-thin material.

"When did you get back?" I tried for a polite, but disinterested tone and failed. Epically. I couldn't hide the breathy lilt of surprise and delight in my voice.

He just smiled in his relaxed, playful way and crossed to the mugs.

"A few hours ago. I hope you'll pardon me. I haven't even had a shower yet."

A mouth-watering image of Daniel standing naked as rivulets of water drew streaks along his dust-covered body washed through the dry canyon of my mind.

Yes, my hands are shaking. This is what happens if a Lilith goes too long without coitus. Mind your business and listen.

My glamour shivered in an unladylike manner.

Daniel grinned again and made himself a mug of tea. He set the ceramic cup gently on the table beside us and turned to face me. He was the only human male in the facility that didn't fear me. Lots of them lusted after me, but they feared me as well.

Poor Daniel. He was either very brave or very stupid.

We stood facing each other under the fizzing fluorescent lights.

The moment stretched the way moments do when more than eyes meet. Daniel's soul flickered inside the blackness of his pupils like a dancing flame. The intoxicating heat of his life-force radiated from his skin.

I stepped closer to his warmth.

What did he see when he looked into my eyes? Did he see the bright, crystal blue irises of my glamour? That enchanted visage of a happy, nerdy, vibrant young woman with just the hint of flirtation pinking her cheeks, pouting her lips, sweeping her thick lashes low over swelling pupils? Or could he see the real me? The sharp, shining silver eyes of the predator I truly was.

"How'd the dig go? Find anything exciting?"

My fingertips brushed the dark hairs on his sun-tanned forearm. I'd never shared my eros with a human before. It was strictly forbidden. Prohibited. Banned. Really, really frowned upon.

My hands travelled up his arms. *Did he notice my warm, syrupy energy pouring over him?* He didn't pull away, so I gave myself permission to roam over his mountain cliff shoulders and down his muscled chest.

This was terribly wrong. Criminal. A violation.

If I kept my touch whisper-soft he might not register the quick graze of nails against his tightening nipples. Daniel's flesh hardened against my circling fingertips.

"A few lower order fossils." He swallowed loudly, looking dazed.

"Intact?"

I distracted him with a palm on his cheek while my other hand traveled to his jeans. I brushed his bottom lip with my thumb and passed my other hand over the swelling bulge beneath his zipper.

"A turtle with all its appendages and v—vertebrae."

His voice dropped to a murmur. He hovered on the sugary sweet edge of surrender.

"Its shell?"

I leaned in and found the dizzy pump of his pulse in his neck. I stretched to my tiptoes and ran my tongue over it.

The fingers of my other hand clamped onto his sideways rod as it lengthened, stretching toward his hip.

Just a quick grasp. Nothing to fight. Nothing to be afraid of. Just keep looking into my eyes.

His skin drank my eros like a parched field.

"Perfect," he breathed.

Blood thundered to all his pulse points making my mouth water. It raced to his shaft, swelling it to an aching hardness beneath my hand. He swayed on his feet as I unzipped his pants and freed his desperate column. It stood at stony attention for me.

I could call his seed with one pump of my hand, but where's the fun in that?

Silence settled over us, a silky quiet that said we'd already spoken everything to each other that needed saying. No need for small talk. There was nothing left but soft submission.

Give yourself to me, Daniel.

For humans, all it took was a lowering of walls, a release of inhibitions, and the connection was made. For fae it was different. Each species had its own rules for courting and mating. Some had no rules at all, only blind instinct.

I wished with all my heart that I could be what Daniel wanted, what he expected from a woman. I wanted to fold into his arms and live happily ever after, but that's not what the Father Who Turned Away had planned for me. I was a monster. A fiendish creature holding his heated cock in my hand.

I looked down at the floor tiles as the weight of my curse settled on my shoulders again.

Trembling fingers brushed my chin as Daniel gently lifted my face to his. Did he fully realize how I'd compromised him? I saw no sense of violation in his gaze.

A thrilling ache filled my stomach. What was the fluttering emotion spreading through my chest? Was it love? I wasn't built for love. I was built for sex. Rough, dangerous, greedy fucking. That's who I was.

The glamour slipped from my eyes like opalescent oil. Daniel's face slackened and his pupils ate the aqua rings of his irises. I pressed into him. I couldn't stop myself. He smelled like man-lust and the ancient hunting grounds of river valleys long past.

The fiery blood of my fore-mothers stirred in my veins. My fingers tightened around his rock-hard pillar. They stretched into smooth black talons.

Stop. Stop!

I just needed a minute to think.

This is Daniel. I can't hurt him.

The warmth of his breath spilled over me and his hands gripped my sides.

Take him! Now!

My eros gushed over us like an ejaculating giant.

The hot, wriggling sexual compulsion of my venereae nature raced to every nerve-ending in my body.

The tingle between my legs swelled to a throbbing tremor.

The last of my glamour slipped from my skin.

Daniel saw the real me. The savage beast made of raging compulsion and violent desire. The soulless succubus with the pointless drive to create and consume. His face slackened with horror and carnal craving.

Desperation spread through me like a wildfire. I hooked my talons and ripped the shirt from Daniel's body.

His skin blushed with succulent vitality. His meaty heart quickened, pounding like a drum, calling to the havoc inside me.

He leaned down and crushed his mouth against mine. His tongue thrust past my teeth begging for me to feast upon it.

It was all I could take. The air crackled around me. The inky strands of my hair brushed my cheeks, swirling in the gravitational confusion.

"Oh God," Daniel whispered under his breath as I pumped his ramrod length with my buzzing palm.

With my other hand, I pushed him backward over the table. I pressed his muscled back against the cool, plastic surface and licked the tendrils of life force from his chest and abdomen. The quivering energy streamed from him in mouthwatering waves, riding his desire.

He didn't struggle as my talons pressed into his skin. He couldn't. I could disembowel him and devour his entrails while he watched and he wouldn't object.

Oh, Goddess, my thoughts echoed his. *Why did he have to come back now? Tonight, when I had so little control. What was wrong with me?*

I needed him. I craved his life force like my lungs hungered for air. I yearned to drink his desire. And, at that moment, I wanted it more than I wanted him to stay alive.

My owl wings transmogrified from the flesh of my back. My favorite sweater dress tore. Mottled feathers sprang from my skin in rapturous release. I climbed on top of Daniel and held him with the metallic flash of my predator eyes. He froze, transfixed.

I straddled his hips and pressed his straining cock against the inner petals of my constricting entrance. Once I fed the head of his shaft into the center of my shuddering garden, it would not let him go. My flesh would devour him, milking him of every ounce of mana he possessed and then it would take more.

"Please," he whispered. The strong, handsome, confident man I'd admired for so long disappeared. The human shivering between my thighs was a pale, desperate shell, mesmerized and helpless.

Yes, I needed release, but not at this cost.

His tea mug slipped from the table and crashed to the floor.

"Daniel," I leaned down to his hungry mouth. His breath thinned to a quick, shallow thread. "I'm sorry." I pressed my lips softly against his and called to Domov.

The air snapped.

The lights blinked.

An emergency aperture chewed through the wall behind me. I leapt from the table and tucked my wings in. The Underhill yanked me backward out of existence.

I didn't fight it.

I covered my face in shame as Daniel and the break room vanished.

My back hit the Underhill's floor, pinning my wings. The smell of sulfur burned my nose. I quickly realized I was not where I'd expected to be.

Instead of a threshold chamber, I found myself in the worst of places.

Hot, heavy air clogged my lungs. Dread crept along my spine like tiny caterpillars as nine council members glared down on me from their semi-circular dais.

The tenth stood over me with his fiery hooves spread wide. Wide enough for me to see straight up his glowing chainmail skirt. Wide enough to behold the wonderland of veins ribbing his legendary cock.

I hated that I couldn't look away from that enormous, flaccid appendage. I loathed the fact that it was attached to the one man I'd rather die than fuck.

"Hi, Hamus." I gave him my best coquettish glance.

He gave me the underside of his massive, sparking hoof.

4

PEG POWLER

"HAG, WATER SPIRIT"

Domain: Corporis
Kingdom: Fae
Phylum: Thantos (death)
Class: Khaos (chaos)
Order: Aqua (water)
Family: Hags
Genus: Grindylow
Species: Really?

I caught the kick before it could break my jaw. But the force of it rang my skull against the stone floor. On an ordinary night, I wouldn't stand a chance against a fae like Hamus, but the delectable drops of Daniel's life force still crackled on my tongue like the popping carbon dioxide candy he'd made me try once.

I swallowed the fizzing bits of handsome paleontologist energy and used the boost to roll free of his attack and scramble to my feet. I stretched my mouth wide to adjust my ears to the depth of the Council Chamber. My head swam in the sudden pressure. Or maybe it was undiluted terror weighing my brain down.

In an instant, I'd been ripped from near sea level to deep into the Earth's crust. At least, I'd been transported the easy way—through a threshold. There was a not so easy way that involved an ancient, empty magma conduit at the center of the Underhill called the Passage of Time. One could take the spiral stairs chiseled into the volcanic tube's walls. Or one could be tossed into the giant tunnel to fall and fall and fall.

Only Old Order fae travelled this deep.

The ruling assembly was made up of ten of the oldest fae still in existence and most of them took the slow way down.

I gasped for breath in the hot, heavy air. Balmy perfection for the fire, rock, and daemon fae. Oppressive for the rest of us.

"Always a pleasure," I rasped.

Hamus shook his head in warning, sparking the embers of his crown. They flickered and smoked. Heat stung me through the torn fabric of my sweater dress. This was not the place for sass, but it was also not the place to show weakness.

There were a lot of dangerous Thantos Phylum fae in the room. Their titanic thoughts grazed my mind. Their destructive gazes frisked my body, seeking frailty, infirmity, defects.

My gut quivered with fear.

Prey behavior like backing down from a seven-foot-tall blazing red bully would stir their aggression and I had the feeling that I was already in enough trouble.

Instead, I dragged my gaze up the length of Hamus' muscular visage seductively. The short skirt of glowing hot chainmail now hid his best feature but still showed a goodly length of muscular thighs.

He took a threatening step toward me.

I lifted my eros-charged fingers which stopped him cold.

Hamus Flamesire, King of the Fire Drakes, was Eros Phylum too but not in a fun times Venereae way. The undiluted eros pumping through his lava veins called to me. It compelled him to procreate the way it compels us all, but he'd shut down his baby-making services after his last wife passed into Greater Life.

I'd heard the tales of his early exploits. Once upon a time, he'd been a passionate lover who'd spawned many lines of compatible fae and a few not so compatible. He'd sired children both in and out of wedlock.

What had gone wrong inside his flaming hot brain? Hamus was way past the time of mourning now. And what was his problem with Venereae? Fae didn't wear scarlet letters, but something told me Hamus would be happy to brand every Venereae in the kingdom.

Starting with me.

I waved the thought away. It didn't matter. No amount of eros would make me spread my legs for that giant specimen of rage and judgement. No matter how perfectly his heavy brows arched. Or how artfully his mouth settled after he spoke. I could live without the ropes of muscle straining across his back. Or the trail of dark hair beckoning down to the thick treasure hanging beneath his glimmering chainmail.

"Do not attempt to enrapture me, Venereae." He forced a chuckle and clomped up the steps of the dais to take his seat with the others. His sooty laugh dirtied the air.

I looked down at my trembling hands. What was wrong with me? Was I going Lilith in the Council Chambers of all places?

"Not a chance," I managed to whisper in response, but the weak retort probably didn't even reach his ears.

Just let me catch you sleeping alone. I'd be happy to go Old Testament on that guy.

It was written in the human scrolls that no unmarried

man could defend against a Lilith if one of my kind found him by himself and asleep. The humans were right, and Hamus was a widower. That counted as single. For human or fae.

Hamus lifted his ashen eyebrows in actual amusement. He may be a few centuries older than me and his fiery Ignis Order might trump my fleshy Carnem Order, but I was scrappy. And hungry. In fact, I would hazard a guess that a few members of the Council might bet on flesh over fire any day.

I looked around at the various fae gathered, and my geneticist's brain began to organize and file. All of the elders were of the Domain Corporis and all were Kingdom Fae. There were pockets of the Underhill that could support non-corporeal beings, but primarily, this was a biome for corporeal fae.

Were-kind and parasitic breeds like vampires could survive in our biome and, for brief amounts of time, so could most humans. But humans were the children of Adam's second wife, Eve, and, as such, belonged to their own taxonomic chart and biome. We fae are the children of Adam's first wife, my namesake, Lilith, and anyone who was strong enough to mate with her.

Poor Adam hadn't stood a chance, but luckily, in the early days, many of the Father's first creations still roamed the world, and they were made of stronger stuff.

Of the council members gathered, only three were Phylum Eros, which was probably a good thing. Too many life energy fae could derail almost any endeavor due to the undeniable pull of creation.

None were my Genus Venereae, which embodied the sex drive, but a couple were of the Flesh Order—Carnem so matters of the flesh were at least represented in some small part. I had a feeling my fate rested in their hands. I certainly hoped it didn't rest in Hamus' volcanic Ignus hands.

Of the fae on the dais that radiated the destructive energy of the Thantos Phylum, several were stronger and older than Hamus. Their death energy seeped through the chamber, crumbling rock and withering bone. A tense balance quivered between the Eros and Thantos.

"I would not have expected to see you brought before us like this, Lilith." A watery voice drew my attention to the far right of the dais.

It was Peg Powler.

I coughed at the sudden skim of fluid building in my chest and quickly averted my gaze. The chill of deep English rivers settled into my bones. The biting cold of still country ponds permeated my heart. It squeezed the muscle. My lungs spasmed.

Peg belonged to the Khaos Class, Aqua Order and was the closest thing I had to a champion on the Council. But I'd crossed a line. Had Peg been a hag of the Greenteeth or Longarms Genera, my Lilith mana could have pushed her Thantos energy from my body. But my luck didn't run that way.

Peg Powler was Genus Grindylow.

Older.

Stronger.

An unparalleled killer.

I'm going down without a fight.

5

CEPHAS STONEFIST

"ROCK ELEMENTAL"

Domain: Corporis
Kingdom: Fae
Phylum: Eros
Class: Ordo (Order)
Order: Lapis (Stone)
Family: Elementals
Genus: Metamorphic
Species: Absolutely not.

"Look at me, child," she gurgled and my head snapped up. Her slime-covered eyes fixed on mine and I suddenly felt like a little girl lost in the misty, English bog of long ago. "You have attacked a human without provocation. Explain yourself."

I stared at Peg in disbelief. The council interrogated, it punished, but it rarely invited one to defend oneself.

I stammered for a moment and then froze when I realized that I didn't have an excuse. I looked around at the council members, trying to hide my panic.

"I…I'm not sure what happened. One minute I was assisting in the Lab and the next…I wasn't feeling like myself."

"And this is when you exited the Underhill?' Councilman Cephas asked. The facets of his gemstone eyes fixed on a place just above and behind my head.

I fought the urge to look over my shoulder.

Cephas and his brother Petros were both Eros phylum, but Cephas was Class Ordo, where his stony twin on the opposite end of the dais was Class Khaos. Cephas valued order above all else, but rock elementals were notoriously disinterested in matters pertaining to the world of flesh. Their minds rolled through the expanse of space and time in a plodding and patient way. The manic inertia that animated fleshy beings perplexed them at best and annoyed them at worst. Blood and bone were ethereal things that ground away beneath the weight of time and stone.

Nonetheless, I could tell that he was after the true details of the event that had just occurred. The same details that spun around my head like scattered marbles.

"Yes, I used a stable threshold overseen by Domov the Clean."

No sooner had I said his name, then the threshold fae appeared behind me. A wavering aperture snapped closed in the wall behind him.

I cupped my face with my hands and turned to meet his shocked gaze.

The clove cigarette I'd given him was lit and hanging from his gaping mouth. It peeled itself from his bottom lip and dropped to the floor.

"A thousand apologies," I whispered through my fingers.

I'd inadvertently used the Old Order fae's full name,

which, for one in a state of servitude, was a summoning. I shook my head and spread my hands wide.

"I'm so sorry, Domov. I used your full name."

His eyes bulged wide as he looked from one councilperson to another.

I'm telling you I've never made that mistake before. No one made that mistake. If I hadn't already been at the bottom of the shaft, I'd have thrown my own self into the Passage of Time.

I covered my face again. I just didn't see Domov as a servant. How could I? He was thousands of years old. I was just twenty-eight—an infant. He was superior to me in every way, but in no way that counted. In the fae order of things, my diminutive friend was genetically a fae-in-thrall. It was his birth right, of sorts, and nothing could change it.

I cringed and turned back to the Council.

Cephas cleared his dusty throat in obvious distress.

"Lilith, refrain from any further speech," he said and my mouth clamped shut.

"Dear Domov," he began calmly, but anger radiated through the cracks in his rocky skin. He took a moment to gather himself and then continued. "We deeply regret this violation and will immediately address the transgression."

"There is no transgression, sir. I am at your service at any hour," Domov answered, but his voice was practically breathless with shock.

"Regardless, we will ensure this never happens again without cause. Please take your leave."

With that, the aperture opened and Domov disappeared in a glimmering swirl of stone.

I lowered my eyes and studied the stunted stalagmites clustered on the floor near my feet. Were they shaking, or was it me?

My sentencing would be swift and the punishment long and agonizing. The penalties handed down by the Council were usually tailored to the family, genus and sometimes specific species of the fae offender.

My mind raced through all the things that would be most painful to me, but, ironically, I was already living my most painful punishments.

No sex.

No children.

"I say, as I have many times before, what good is a Lilith to a breeding program?" Hamus's words dripped with the magma of his hatred.

I raised my gaze to him. What lurked in our past that had led to this level of loathing? Hamus wasn't exactly the warm and cuddly type. No fae from the Daemon Family were. He was Draco genus as well, which hardened his shell even further, but dragons and owls weren't natural enemies. What had I done to piss him off so badly?

"Let me burn her to ash and we can be done with this," Hamus's eyes flared a dangerous orange and flames danced to life between his fingers.

Cephas raised a boulder hand and crashed it down on the table. Sparks slid across the obsidian surface, but it did not crack.

My head was another story. I clamped my hands over my ears, reeling from the deafening sound. The pressure released from my body as the ancient eyes of the Council turned from me to Cephas.

"Hamus, does not your name mean 'father of a multitude?' The Daemon Family should be filled to overflowing by now. Where is the Draco Genus in the Book of Bones? Near extinction." Cephas asked and answered his own questions. "This Lilith has put her eros to good use. She has wooed many rare specimens to our program."

I couldn't be sure, but it felt as though the temperature in the cavern spiked a few degrees. My thoughts floated in the stifling warmth. I looked to Peg, but if she was uncomfortable in the sweltering heat, she didn't show it. The thin layer of water that clung to her bluish-gray skin was still and calm.

"Brother, there are other…elements to consider." Petros spoke this time. He was the mirror of Cephas, but for the streaks of lichen that stained his stony face. The dark green tears ran from his eyes to stripe his craggy cheeks.

The only other thing that distinguished the two was the mantle of moss on his brother Cephas's shoulders. It gave the older brother an air of royalty though both were great-grandsons of the First Wife.

The other members of the Council gave a nod of agreement.

"Perhaps some time away from the Underhill, would be…refreshing for Lilith," Peg's voice hissed like steam through the heated air.

My mouth fell as far open as it could without my jaw unhinging.

The council members exchanged glances that held more in them than I could read. All except Hamus, who continued to glare at me with withering orange eyes.

A silence followed that stretched so long, I thought, at one point, that I could hear the heartbeat of the world somewhere below my feet.

"Lilith," Cephas's voice broke the silence in a chorus of grinding rocks. "You are hereby granted two weeks of paid vacation. You may spend it however you wish. Please exit the Underhill within the hour."

I barely had time to blink before a threshhold ground to life on the wall behind me and I was sucked away. I tumbled onto the cold stone of my bedroom and lay there in a shivering heap while my body attempted to decompress.

The cooler air chilled the sweat on my skin as I kicked free of my damp, torn dress.

"What just happened?" I whispered up at the stony ridges stretching diagonally across my ceiling. The enormous corrugation of rock was only a tiny piece of the Underhill's vertebral column. I'd seen other pieces of its backbone in the upper laboratories. Sometimes ribs appeared in the common areas several levels down, but no one had seen enough of the mountain's skeleton to form a full picture of its anatomy. I'm pretty sure even the Underhill didn't know what its true form was.

"Why am I not dead?"

The Locus Geographia said nothing. Not even a tremor to acknowledge I'd spoken.

One minute, I'd been bracing for a painful month or two in the Wells with the Soul Seepers and their endlessly creative devices of torture, and the next minute, I—I was headed out on vacation?

Had Cephas defended me? Cephas, the impenetrable obelisk of primordial stone? Cephas, the councilman least concerned with creatures of flesh? Cephas, the most likely to crush a petitioner than hear their plea?

And what had Petros been talking about when he'd mentioned other elements? I blinked in confusion, guilt, and gob-smacked relief.

Daniel's okay. If he wasn't, I'd be in the Wells.

I glanced around at my messy space. Did I even own a suitcase?

I stood and walked to my closet. I numbly grabbed a sundress from its hanger and threw it on my bed.

I'd already made up my mind.

Florida.

Fuck it all. If I'm going on vacation…I'm going on vacation.

6

PONYTAIL MOM

"FELINE, HUMAN HYBRID"

Domain: Corporis (corporeal)
Kingdom: Human
Phylum: Eros (life)
Class: Ordo (order)
Order: Primate
Family: Hominidae/Feles (humanoid cats)
Genus: Silvestris (wildcat)
Species: Soccer Mom

Suburbia stared me down from its curtained windows and painfully manicured gardens. It was a veritable oasis to the human eye, but to me it was a weeping world.

The pesticides in the grass practically foamed in my mouth. I stood on the curb, clutching a brightly wrapped birthday present and eyeing my old college roommate's emerald green lawn of death.

The collection of tempered steel minivans and SUVs in her driveway made my ears ring.

The hotel shuttle pulled away behind me, trailing Latin music down the street. Birds chirped. Lawn mowers purred, and all around me the high-pitched, seagull sweet screeches of human children drifted on the summer air. It was the happiest of sounds.

I took a deep breath and adjusted my glamour. It had taken two extra hours in the crowded Fae Travel Visa Office inside Miami International Airport, but I'd passed the inspections.

Florida, as you probably know, is a Glamour Intact state—meaning all fae with the capability to appear human are ordered by law to do so.

Of the three types of states, I much preferred Glamour Intact ones.

Glamourless States—which, thankfully, there were only a few—prohibited all visual artifice. So, if I had to chase down a desert fae in say Utah or Nevada, I had to do it al fresco with all my not so dainty Lilith features on full display.

They shoot at fae in Utah. Just sayin'.

I know it's hard to understand what glamourless feels like. Have you ever visited a nudist colony? It's kind of like that.

The third type, Glamour Apparent states, *which some of you are probably from*, were mostly in the middle of the country and allowed glamours, but only if they were apparent.

It's tough to hold your glamour a few centimeters off your body so the rainbow of charms are constantly showing. *You don't believe me? Try holding your makeup a smidge off your face.*

Now, shush. You're distracting me.

Glamoured up or not, I hadn't seen my college roommate in four years, and I needed a vacation. This was Florida, the perfect place for humans to get away and unwind. I'm sure it worked for fae as well.

The door of the two-story transitional in front of me burst open and children spilled onto the lawn in a soggy, cake-smeared riot.

An errant water balloon broke free of the melee and caught me squarely on the shoulder. The slap of rubber against my skin jarred me, sending a ripple through my glamour.

"Oh no!" A wind chime voice sounded from the porch. "Boys! What do you say?"

"Sorry," the cake-smeared chorus replied.

The parade of birthday party children made a hard right and disappeared around the corner of the house.

I smiled and shrugged at the golden-haired woman on the porch.

"Always in the wrong place at the wrong time," she giggled, trotting down the driveway. "I can't believe you're here in Coral Gables," she sang and wrapped her arms around me. "I missed you." Dalia took the gift from me and squeezed me again.

I was still getting used to the idea that my college cohort had a child, much less one that was turning seven years old today.

"I missed you too," I said, breathing in the fruity scent of her hair.

Dalia's "hippy-dippy" regime of non-toxic hair and beauty supplies had made it so much easier for me to share a dorm room with her. From the smell of her, nothing had changed in that department.

"I swear, your glamour looks exactly the same. Which means you haven't aged a day," she exclaimed, clamping the gift under her arm and cupping my face.

"The only good thing about being fae, I guess." I

shrugged, then glanced at the house. "Are your guests okay with having a 'night monster' in their midst?"

"Of course." She winked.

Dalia was what we fae called a "touchy-feely" human. In college, I'd grown used to her constant tactile sensing. She ran her hands through my hair approvingly.

"Just like water through my fingers," she cooed.

I knew from our sorority days that Dalia was different from other human females. Usually, non-fae women maintained precise physical boundaries with other women unless they were initiating sexual contact. Dalia had never played by the rules and hadn't expected me to either. It was a human/fae match made in heaven.

I wished we hadn't let life push us apart after grad school.

"Come on in." She took my hand. "I'll show you around. Jeez, Lil, it's a hundred degrees out here and you're as cold as ice. Some things never change."

I automatically thought to make excuses about the shuttle's air-conditioning being on full blast and then I remembered, *this is Dalia.* She knows almost everything a human could about a member of the fae. There were some things, darker things, that I'd strategically left out of our orientation meeting at college, but she knew the important stuff:

No sex with men in our dorm room.

No sex with women in our dorm room.

No sex with me in our dorm room unless she wanted to die.

Dalia had signed up for the human/fae relations program early on and she'd been the one that picked me as a roommate.

I smiled as she dragged me up the driveway.

This was exactly what I needed, time away from the lab, away from the fae, away from being Field Agent Lilith Nightkin of Hans Jodkins University's Center for Functional Anatomy and Evolution or FAE.

I just needed to be Lil for a while.

Two lemonades and a few socially awkward attempts to blend later, I still felt like an ink stain standing there on the sun-dappled patio in my dark burgundy sun dress with my black hair hanging loose. I wished I'd braided my hair into a bun or at least adjusted my glamour to appear as though I had even the slightest tan.

I wasn't sure if Dalia had clued anyone in to my particular faeness, but from the stray looks and nervous body-language, I was figuring she had.

The backyard party was made up mostly of preadolescent children and a smattering of mothers. Each mom was lovelier than the next in their brightly-colored workout clothes and seamless tans.

"So, Dal says you're a scientist," the young mother with the bouncy ponytail offered in an attempt to break the ice. She looked at me as though I had a third eye protruding from my forehead, but I appreciated the attempt at conversation. I'd been living and working around humans for years, yet I still managed to give off the unmistakable stink of social awkwardness.

"Yes, um, I'm a geneticist."

Well, I am—kind of. I have a BA in Molecular Biology and an MS in Human Genetics. No, I don't have a MD. Why do you ask? Are you writing my biography?

"Wow, with DNA and stuff?"

"Mmhmm."

"Oh, how interesting." She smiled as her voice trailed off. I pursed my lips together and smiled back.

"So, which one is yours?" I asked, pointing to the knot of children.

"The one with the sandy blond curls. I know his hair is too long. It makes him look like a girl, but the curls are so cute, I can't bear to cut them."

Ponytail Mom beamed. I couldn't help but beam with her. But my thoughts conjured the image of a child much different from her cherub-faced boy.

I pictured a raven-haired girl with mercury eyes and soft, downy wings folded against her thin back.

Then, the image changed.

A scarlet-skinned boy with lava eyes and a dusting of iridescent dragon scales appeared in my mind's eye.

Oh, Goddess!

Where had he come from?

I'd pictured what my daughter might look like many times before, but never how a son might appear. If a Lilith had a girl child—as my mother had—the baby would be almost identical to her matriarch. But if a Lilith mated with a full-blooded fae of another genetic family, the child would resemble the father completely.

Other fae families could combine genes like humans do, but not Liliths. Our DNA was crazy that way.

My stomach knotted.

Did that small vision mean there was a flame-haired child with cloven feet and a tinder bright smile waiting in my future? After one hundred of my other children had met a bloody end?

My thoughts snapped back to my immediate surroundings.

"No, definitely don't cut those curls," I agreed a little breathlessly.

She smiled again, turning luminescent eyes to me.

There, that's how you do it, Lil. Small talk. Focus on the children. The real children. Not the ones that will never be.

"Do you have kids?" Ponytail Mom asked, looking around.

"Oh no, haven't met the right guy yet."

My smile faltered.

She must have seen the disappointment in my eyes, because she returned the smile and said, "It'll happen. You're so pretty. I know it'll happen soon."

"Thanks."

She gave me a friendly nod and bounced down the yard to help the other moms settle the children around the reptile show.

"Liam loves the water-gun," Dalia professed and sank into the lawn-chair next to me. "You didn't have to bring him a present."

She pointed to the chair next to her and I happily joined her.

Dalia's yard stretched away from us into the torturously manicured distance. In the far back, the landscaping sloped gently down to a sparkling waterway where her husband was overseeing the main event.

We watched as the vendor, Mr. Rattles, handed her husband a boa constrictor.

"Jim's sure being a good sport about the snakes," I said, trying not to giggle.

Dalia's husband looked one shade short of terrified, but he followed the snake guy's instructions and draped the pale-yellow boa around his neck.

"Yeesh." Dalia cringed as she watched the snake curling around him. "Liam's been into reptiles for a couple of years now. He's been begging us for a pet corn snake. It isn't that I mind them that much. This is South Florida after all, but—yeah, I baked the cake—Jim can hold the snake."

This time we both giggled.

"So, you're here for a whole two weeks?" she asked.

I loved how she sprinkled her voice with mischief sometimes. It always promised good things. We hadn't had real girl time since the ski trip four years ago.

"Yes, two whole weeks, no lab, no thinking about work at all. Just cocktails and sandy beaches," I assured her.

As I said it, I realized that I hadn't thought about work in several hours. Usually, by now, I would have calculated the genetic make-up of every guest at this party.

Now that I'd thought of it, none of the adults seemed to be above a .001 mixture of fae blood except, oddly, for Ponytail Mom. The rusty specks on her otherwise denim blue eyes were congregating around her pupils in a roughly diamond shape. That indicated a pre-emergence of any of the feline fae.

I'd need a blood sample to be sure. If her offspring chose well, she could be the proud great grandmother of a Scottish Cat Sith.

"Lil?" Dalia had her mom face on. "Were you just thinking about work?"

"No! Well, yes, but not now."

"Take a deep breath," she instructed.

I did.

I pulled the plug on the genetic server whirring to life in my head and let my body melt into the chair.

"Smell the mimosa. Listen to the breeze in the palm trees and just relax."

I closed my eyes and unclenched. I was in real danger of actually relaxing. Thankfully, a blood-curdling scream tore the soft summer serenity in two.

7

LESSER NAGA

"HYBRID SERPENT, PARTY-CRASHER"

Domain: Corporis
Kingdom: Unknown, suspected Fae
Phylum: Unknown
Class: Unknown
Order: Reptilia (reptile)
Family: Serpentes (snakes)
Genus: Naga
Species: Your guess is as good as mine.

Both our heads whipped toward the source of the scream. Down at the water's edge, it was as if a bomb had gone off in the middle of the happy, little reptile show. Chairs flew through the air. Children shrieked.

Jim stood frozen in place with the fat, yellow boa still draped on his shoulders. I followed his stricken stare to something on the table just behind Mr. Rattles. It hissed over the piercing screams of a mother as she scrambled to reach her child.

There, atop a large, shattered glass tank coiled an even larger snake.

Dalia sucked in a breath. Mr. Rattles staggered back. Jim launched the boa.

Fear's a funny thing.

Do I feel fear?

Sure.

Did I want to run from the giant, menacing serpent swaying in the dappled light of Dahlia's lawn?

No.

Remember, I'm Chaos Class. When most people think "chaos," their minds conjure up bedlam, confusion, a riotous lack of order. They're not wrong. The energetic signature of the force known as chaos does cause disarray. It often results in mayhem. It is by its very nature disordered. But it's so much more than that. Chaos is the primordial drive to sunder, to rend, to deconstruct. It is the grinding darkness that snuffs out stars. It is the fire and the ash. It is the blade and the cleaving. It is what the universe was before creation splintered it.

Did I want to run?

Yes.

Toward it.

What remained of the tank's metal frame collapsed under the weight of the hulking reptile, and I wondered how it had ever fit inside such a small space. Its wide, muscular body bunched and its short tail blurred as it shook its stubby rattle.

The creature swung its massive head toward the scattering crowd, and a splash of sunlight illuminated its blunt profile. It turned almost humanoid facial features toward the gaping reptile vendor. A greenish-brown hood the size of a golf umbrella spread from its neck on either side.

Jim hesitated for a heartbeat then dove for Mr. Rattles just as the enormous snake coiled to strike. Its mammoth body launched forward as Jim tackled Mr. Rattles around the legs. The creature sliced through the air toward the unfortunate man's head, but just missed him with its outstretched fangs.

Jim and Mr. Rattles went down together. The former football player still had skills. I'd seen Jim make tackles like that in college.

The snake crashed onto the lawn in a knot of picnic blankets and more screams.

I was up and running as it wriggled free, but as I dodged the fleeing crowd, I caught a glimpse of its undercarriage.

I lost my balance and crashed into a pile of folding chairs, which sent me tumbling to a stop almost right beneath it. There, camouflaged in the pale, greenish-white skin of its abdomen was a set of small, but muscular arms.

It tracked me with its sideways stare as I scrambled to get my feet under me.

It's easy to assign emotions to animals, particularly when their facial anatomy seems built into a natural grimace, but there was no mistaking the expression on this thing's face…it was pissed. And it was definitely not just an animal.

It reared up in front of me and locked eyes in a way that lower order creatures don't. Behind me, Jim shouted orders, and farther away, Dalia called to me in a voice gone thin with fear. The creature leaned forward and its forked tongue flicked at the air between us, bright red and glistening.

It drew in breath and its lips parted.

"Sssssstranger," it hissed in a voice that crept around my neck and tightened. "Concccceealer of flesh."

I leapt to my feet with one word in my head.

Naga.

There was a naga in my best friend's backyard. It flicked its tongue at me again and I punched it. Hard. The naga's furious head whirled around.

Dripping fangs extended from the roof of its wide mouth, and my chaos took a step back. The violent buzzing of its rattle shook the confidence out of me. I'd never seen a real naga before, but I'd read Dr. Sampson's paper on the morphological integration of secondary fae anatomy with reptilian species. His fossil records were almost identical to this creature, but they had been much smaller.

This was no watered-down genetic remnant of a long extinct fae. Nor was it one of the semi-divine beings of Hindu and Buddhist origin. Those creatures could be dangerous, but mostly they were described as beneficent and uncommonly beautiful. The creature in front of me, coiling to strike again, was nothing more than a brute with the power of speech.

Its undulating body sprang at me. I caught it by its hood, clamping my hands down hard on the fanned ridge to either side of its head. Its eyes widened in shock. It swept at my legs with its tree trunk tail, but I'd spread my feet wide.

"Where did you come from?" I stared into its glittering pupils as it turned one eye and then the other toward me. It collapsed its hood and lunged for my face.

I locked my arms and dug my fingers into its warm and surprisingly smooth skin. It missed my face, but I'd left my arms vulnerable. It whipped its mouth sideways and spread its fangs wide. I released my grip, but there was no getting my arm out of the way in time. Instead, I lifted my knee into the space between us just as its fangs pierced my skin.

Fire tore at my arm as I planted my foot on its chest.

The naga's strong arms reached for my ankle, but it was too late. I applied some full-blooded fae strength and kicked it off Dalia's property and half away across the waterway. It landed with a huge splash.

The gasps and shouts renewed behind me as the party-goers clambered for the safety of Dalia's sunroom.

Jim stood only feet away from me. Terror tightened his handsome face as he scanned the waterway, but he hadn't run.

"Are you okay?" he asked hesitantly. His breath was as shallow as a summer puddle. Jim knew I wasn't a daughter of Eve, but he'd always treated me like a lady, and I appreciated it.

"Yes…I think so," I answered calmly, hiding my arm behind me. The pain pulsing from the puncture wounds lit a fuse inside me. That snake had my attention. Fae or not, it was coming with me. All of it. Or pieces of it.

Its choice.

"Come on. Let's get away from the water. I'll call animal control." Jim took off running toward the house.

I clamped my hand over the shallow puncture wounds on my arm and applied pressure. The naga's venom sizzled beneath my skin. It burned like a bright, beautiful brushfire.

Thankfully, it hadn't gotten a good grip on me. If it had, I'd have six-inch naga fangs impaling my forearm now. That's a fast way to lose an arm, even a fae one.

Pain. *Good.*

Dismemberment. *Bad.*

All around me, tiny corn-snakes leaked from overturned tanks. Their brightly-colored bodies wound through the grass at Mr. Rattles' feet. His hands dug knuckle deep into his hair as he surveyed his ruined display.

I walked calmly over to the wide-eyed man. His face slackened with disbelief.

"Hey." I snapped my fingers in front of him, but he didn't even notice me. "Hey!" I let go of my arm and waved a bloody hand in his face. Mr. Rattles looked from his display to the widening ripples leading down the waterway. He took a step back from me and my arm shot out.

I held the man by the front of his sweat-soaked tee-shirt.

"Look at me," I demanded, but his peripheral nervous system was playing keep away with his attention.

I twisted my fist into the fabric, including just enough chest hair to cut through the panic and make him focus on me. His eyes snapped back to my face. He shook his head from side to side.

"Where did you get that snake?" I whispered through gritted teeth so he'd have to lean in.

He blinked at me, trying to fit me into the destruction that only moments ago had been his exhibit. The yard had emptied out except for the snakes and lizards that now slithered and crept toward freedom across the lawn.

"G—get off me," he said, grabbing my hand. The chill of my skin must have shocked him because his gaze shot back to my eyes. I dropped just enough glamour from my face for him to see the black sclera surrounding my silver irises.

"Woah, what's wrong with your eyes?" He abandoned his chest hair and stepped back far enough that his tee-shirt ripped.

"Where—did—you—get—that—snake?" I let the points of my real teeth show.

His sun-beaten face went slack with fear.

"In—in the watershed."

"The Everglades cover a lot of land. Where exactly?"

"Look, I don't want any trouble. I'll totally refund you." His voice squeaked like a dog toy. I shook him until his teeth rattled.

"Off of Tamiami Trail. Big Cypress Swamp. By the Reservation. There's a bunch of them. It was injured, hit by a car, I think. I—I thought it was one of those giant salamanders people been releasing in the Glades. They're not supposed to be mean," he blurted, "or talk."

I had literally no response to that so we just stared at each other for a second. I let go of his shirt and he fell backward onto the ground.

The naga had a huge head start, but I could still smell him.

"What are you?" Mr. Rattles asked as he crab-crawled away from me.

I replaced my glamour and turned back to him.

"What do you mean?" I blinked human eyes at him.

His mouth moved soundlessly. I stepped over him and began the hunt.

8

FREE-RANGE PIXIE

"SOUTHERN RIDGED-WING VARIANT"

Domain: Corporis
Kingdom: Fae/Human
Phylum: Eros
Class: Ordo
Order: Insecta (insect)
Family: Pixie
Genus: Tropicus (tropical)
Species: Avocado?

Murky canal water sloshed against the bulkhead at the end of Dalia's yard. The dark waterway held barely a trace of the aqua beauty of the ocean only a mile away and none of its transparency. Luckily, the canal wasn't deep or particularly wide. I watched the water's surface as I ran.

A few blocks up, the waterway narrowed and turned left into a golf course. I kept an eye on the golfers as I checked a few ponds that spilled out of the waterway to create hazards for the course. A pond with an angry naga in it was probably more hazard than the average golfer needed.

I hurried along as the water straightened and narrowed. I now had a line of sight for about six blocks ahead of me, but still no naga. I could tell that it was moving west because its faintly pungent scent clung to the surface of the sluggish water.

After the next bend in the canal, I had a clear shot at eight to ten more blocks. I set a brisk pace and scanned the rippling surface. When I cleared the next bend, I saw it.

The naga wriggled from the water and slithered into a thin stand of trees lining the canal on the right. I was on the left bank so I took a quick look around and, seeing no one, I leapt across the water.

As a Lilith, I have some control over my body's relationship with gravity. I wasn't a flying fae, nor did I have some fae's ability to hover, but I damn sure could leap. Even so, I still made a bit of noise when I hit the other side as my left foot slipped and splashed into the water.

"Damn!" There went my best sandals. Italian leather with a real wooden heel.

Now I'm pissed.

The naga's head whipped around at the sound and hissed. As soon as it saw me, it dove back into the water. I moved to pursue, but something small and dark green caught my eye. Wobbly wings fluttered past me, fighting the breeze.

Without a closer look, a human might dismiss it as a butterfly, but my demi-owl eyes fixed on the buttery green head and pencil-thin body of the pixie just as it realized its mistake. Free-range pixies were stringy from all the exercise, but their bones were crunchier and their flavors really popped.

The tiniest squeak emanated from it as I plucked it from the air. Its dark green wings were trimmed in brown and its spindly legs ended in curly brown toes. My mouth watered. I'd heard about the tropical fruit-flavored pixies of the southern-most states.

Was this a guava pixie? Or maybe a lime?

I tossed the unexpected treat in my mouth and crunched until its insides exploded on my tongue. *Avocado. And not even ripe. Gross.* Energy flooded through me.

If it had been night, I could have taken owl form, and the naga would have been in my talons before the next bend, but the sun's energy diffused my powers.

I thanked the Night Mother for the pixie boost—however yucky. Even if I could take my night form, this wreaking snake wasn't worth taking a chance on revealing myself to humans. Eve's children were well-behaved until they felt threatened. An owl-woman with an eleven-foot wingspan and dagger-sharp talons wasn't what they wanted to see racing through the heart of their Glamour Intact community.

The next five or six blocks were tree-lined and backed up to an industrial area. I put on speed and calculated my intercept. As the naga wove through another bend, it began to break for air more often.

Getting tired already?

Up ahead, the canal widened into a retention pond. If I timed it right, I could reach the other side of the pond where the water bottle-necked under a foot bridge and continued on. I could use the bridge to launch myself in front of it.

The naga risked a glance back as it broke for air and then it put on a burst of speed.

The trees thinned and ended at the mouth of the pond and that's when it all went wrong.

I slammed on the brakes as I crashed through the last of the trees and tumbled into a small parking lot.

Blackness swarmed my vision. I lost all sensory input. I

gripped my skull. I'd gone completely head blind. Rainbows swam around me as my glamour wavered.

I tumbled forward and my dress tore as I hit the cement. My shoulder scraped along a curb and the strap of my sandal snapped, flinging my shoe from my foot. I came to a stop in a crumpled heap half on and half off the curb.

I threw my hands out in front of me protectively. Cars screamed by. Slicing sports cars. Bruising buses. Sucker punching SUVs. Their engines sucked poison and pumped it through their metal veins. Their venomous vapors belched into the silky Florida breeze clogging my lungs.

The freeway.

It wasn't a foot bridge the naga was darting under. *That's an off-ramp.* I must have been so hyper-focused that I'd missed the increase in defilement.

I checked for injuries as I pulled myself to the relative safety of a grassy embankment. Tanker trucks whizzed past me. A medical center fizzed on the other side of the parking lot I'd fallen into.

Hospitals are something for which I usually needed to prepare. Back at Hans Jodkins, the Underhill was as far from the Radiology Department as possible, but even so, I was able to adjust my vibration to block it out. Even highways with their septic cement and toxic metal didn't usually affect me like this. *What had pummeled me so hard?*

I blinked until my focus sharpened and I took a look around. I saw the pond, the off-ramp, the highway, and the bleeding rips the cars left in the air as they tore past. I saw the medical center and the warped aura of twisted molecules that clung to it.

I stood, brushed myself off, and grabbed my shoe.

That naga's head is going to look great hanging on my wall, I thought.

I took a few steps toward the off-ramp the canal ran

under as it hugged the side of the freeway. That's when I felt it. Fresh, searing pain sizzled through my skull. I clamped my hands on either side of my head and staggered to a bench at the front of the parking lot.

I focused on the agony behind my forehead and visualized a box around it. I shrank the box until it was small enough to not get in my way. I moved my head from side to side until I could get a bearing on the source of the pain. I squinted through the sunlight at the darkened underpass and the intersection just beyond it.

There it was. A Swifty Lube.

Son of a bitch.

The over-charged electric fence containing the critical care cars crackled with menace. Power lines surged from a back building to an onsite auto-wash, then over to the main garage and back again, forming a triangle. A closed trine. The warped energy with no outlet pulsed and pressed at my aura.

Humans and their dead heads.

Trines might not cause them pain as they did fae-kind, but I'd bet a goblet of steaming hot pixie blood the mechanics that worked inside that business were practically homicidal.

I took a moment to assess my situation while I expelled the Swifty Lube toxins. I was hours into my lovely Florida vacation and chasing a mythical creature through a densely populated human biome.

Arm bleeding.

Shoulder stinging.

Sandal broken.

Brand new sundress torn.

And a specimen running from me.

So, a normal day, all in all. At least I hadn't lost my phone.

I pulled the burled wood, battery-dampening case that

housed my cell from the pocket of my dress and punched in Dalia's number. My side of the conversation went like this:

"Hi…I'm not sure…It's a medical center up the street a ways…no I'm fine…I just tripped…No, I'm really fine, just scraped up a little…I know, but I just wanted to get a look at that weird snake thing…not sure…Are the kids okay?… Curiosity is an occupational hazard for me…no, it swam away…I've already ordered a car to pick me up…yes…I'm just going to head back to the hotel…I'm really tired…Is Jim okay? Good…yep, always exciting…See you later."

Jim had already called Animal Control. I made a mental note to check with their office to see if they had received any other calls about strange snake behavior. According to Mr. Rattles, there could be a nest of those things out there just waiting to ruin the tourist trade.

I picked myself up, dusted off, and headed for the off-ramp. I followed the canal as it squeezed under the freeway. A few blocks down, the murky waterway flooded into the Everglades. I left the motorized mayhem behind and started off into the wild and welcoming watershed.

9

HUMAN/NAGA HYBRID

"SNAKE EYES"

Domain: Corporis
Kingdom: Human
Phylum: Unknown
Class: Unknown
Order: Primates/Reptilia
Family: Hominidae/Serpentes
Genus: Homo/Pythonidae
Species: Sapiens/Reticulatus

I picked up the naga's trail about fifty yards out as it thrashed through the soggy underbrush. It slithered in a westerly direction, travelling parallel to the Tamiami Trail.

I'd done a little research on the area before I'd left Maryland. The Florida Everglades were one of the last remote wildernesses of the United States and came highly recommended by both fae and human friends alike.

I plunged into the scrubby marshland. The wiry

sawgrass sizzled in the late afternoon sun. This part of the Everglades was a wasteland, unbuildable, unusable, inhospitable.

"Paradise."

Back in the birth time of the Fae, when our numbers poured forth from Adam's first wife, the first of her daughters —the Liliths—lived in the wild and barren places. The Kabbalah describes the Liliths as having been condemned to walk those lonely desert lands.

What did those dummies know about our true nature?

A place of chaos, tangled root and fractured earth just felt —right. It energized me. I took a deep breath and pulled that sacred vibration into my body.

My phone dinged with the text I had been waiting for. I'd promised myself I wouldn't call the office while on vacation, but a party-crashing naga changes things. With dwindling cell phone reception, I'd texted Daphne and asked her to check the Book of Bones for North American naga colonies. I'd hesitated to contact her until I knew more. Undocumented fae in the contiguous states would surely have her dryad branches in a bunch, but I needed to know what I was up against.

I wanted to ask about Daniel too, but an owl pellet of fear the size of my fist had lodged itself in my windpipe. What if the answer was no?

The text conversation went like this:

"I double-checked. No naga sightings outside of the Himalayas. The last sightings were a century ago. Do u need back up?"

"No, I think I can handle it. It might be a weakened, genetic reemergence, but I'm not sure."

"Be careful. Reptilian mixed breeds have unpredictable behavior. It could be aggressive."

"Yeah, I got that." I checked the pulsing bite on my arm.

The bleeding had finally slowed to a clearish-pink trickle. Probably due to an anticoagulant in its venom.

"Do u have a sample kit?"

"I'm on vacation. Why would I pack a sample kit?"

"This is me ur talking 2."

"Fine. Yes, I've got a kit, but it's at the hotel. I'm tracking a fading scent so gotta go."

"Bring me back that blood! Tissue 2!"

"I'll c what I can do."

"Also, if that human was correct in believing that there are more, u might be looking for a Naga-Loka. Naga colonies are described as resplendent, underground palaces similar to Underhills. With the water table being what it is down there, I might look for a mound or elevated earthen structure."

"Got it. Thanks."

"Be careful."

"Will do." I stuffed my phone back in my pocket and slung my sandals over my shoulder. I took another deep breath, inhaling the wild and indifferent chaos that infused the land.

This vacation just got a whole lot better.

I smelled the Naga-Loka before I saw it.

An early evening storm bubbled to life on the western horizon. It pushed the briny scents of salt marshes and the citrus sweet smell of fruit tree farms across the watery landscape. I'd enjoyed the tropical fragrances as I'd made my way through the brittle, buzzing wetlands, but the wind shifted.

The pungent odor of animal feces, dirty bodies, and decay rolled over me.

I'd found the Naga-Loka despite Mr. Rattles' vague directions. *By the reservation*, hadn't been the most specific description he could have given. I'd already encountered three separate reservations, none of which had a naga problem.

The fourth, however, was riddled with them.

I crept toward the isolated community, keeping low to the soggy ground. No roads connected to this settlement, which sat atop a large round hummock of solid earth set deep into the swampland. A system of canals surrounded the circular parcel of land creating a virtual island in the middle of the marsh.

I caught the scent of both human and naga as the wind picked up ahead of the storm. Slowly, I altered my course from due west to a more southwestern direction until the first buildings came clearly into view.

Sturdy trees lifted from the flat, brushy expanse of the watershed like sentinels standing at attention around the curved edge of the island. Pale bits of grass clung to the rounded earth as it climbed upward in a mound formation. Maybe a hundred small huts crowded around the top of the mound in a messy circle three and four deep, leaving the center of the rise empty except for a thin ring of stones.

I crept closer for a better look.

The stones encompassed a large, round hole roughly four or five feet across. It could have been a well, but as the wind turned again, I could smell it wasn't. By the stench of it, this entire hill was a Naga-Loka and I'd just found the entrance.

I waited, still as a corpse, in a cluster of trees at the edge of the reservation as the storm swept in. Tall thunderclouds reached across the sky blanketing the wetlands in shadow. Long bolts of lightning probed the barren landscape. Fat, stinging rain dropped from the icy heights to cool the steaming ground.

The tiny, insubstantial houses huddled together under

their thatched roofs like plump, gray mice. Delicious mice. Mice that were blissfully unaware of the owl watching them.

Rainbows danced before my eyes as my glamour wobbled. The minute I stepped foot on that reservation, I would no longer be in American territory. No glamour laws applied.

What little activity there was outside came to a stand-still as the residents ran for shelter.

I waited.

I considered the reasons why a community of humans might share their home with a non-human species like the naga. I guess there was the possibility that they didn't know of the nagas' presence, but everything about the arrangement of the settlement suggested otherwise.

Was there a history here of symbiosis between humans and fae? There were small enclaves of hybrid culture that had evolved together in other parts of the world even before the Revelation twenty years ago. Some Welsh and Cornish communities have quietly shared their lives with the fae for centuries. Had such a society developed here at the farthest tip of the United States, practically underneath the Council's noses?

I took my phone from my pocket and snapped a few pictures of the settlement.

A small child scampered from one hut to the next. Before entering the second dwelling, it turned and looked in my direction. I thought to duck, but humans didn't have good enough eye-sight to pick out shapes at that distance. I, on the other hand, had exceptional sight thanks to my species.

Oh, did you think I was going to tell you my species? Nope. I wasn't.

I peered through the rain at the little human's face. Dark hair plastered to her soft, round features and pouting lips, but as I looked closer—there was something unusual about her eyes. She tilted her head as she glanced my way, and a look a fear washed over her. The slits of her pupils widened with fright. Humans didn't have slits. Snakes had slits.

I put my finger to my lips in the sign of silence and let a bit of my glamour fall away.

Color drained from the kid's face as she backed into the next hut and disappeared. She'd definitely seen me.

I'd need blood samples from the humans as well. From now on, I'd stuff a sample kit in my bra. A girl never knew when she would have to bleed someone or take a chunk of flesh.

The minutes dragged by as I waited for the height of the storm. No other humans appeared. The child must have kept quiet. Smart kid.

The clouds above thickened into a slate wall, and warm, glowing lights flickered to life inside the huts. This was as dark as it was going to get before the storm moved out. Nightfall wasn't far away, but I couldn't wait for full dark to transmogrify into my owl form and storm the stinky castle. If the naga did have friends, he'd had plenty of time to warn them of my pursuit.

I closed my eyes and dropped my glamour.

Rain hammered down, flattening my sundress to my pale blue skin. My hair turned to a liquid curtain of night, clinging to my breasts, flowing over my shoulders, and spilling down to my hips. I licked the fresh rain from my blood red lips. A sharp-toothed grin spread across my face.

Just a few snakes down a dark hole.

Fun!

10

NAGA LOKA

"MALODOROUS HOLE IN THE GROUND"

Domain: Corporis
Kingdom: Unknown
Phylum: Eros
Class: Ordo
Order: Calcitite (limestone particulate)
Family: Histosol (organic soil)
Genus: Marl (algal detritus)
Species: Muck. Very smelly. I mean—horrendous.

Feathers itched beneath my skin waiting for release. The storm hid the coming sunset from view, but the last desperate rays of its energy held me in my current form. Daylight grew all things, but the night ate them. The night ate everything. There was no creation without chaos. I hugged my ribs and scratched at my back.

Soon, I told myself. Soon, the darkness would unzip my frail skin and free my true essence. My body prepared for it like the final lick of a lover's tongue. But I couldn't wait. The chase had teased the chaos in me to a mindless froth. My instincts dragged me through the quiet village, all the way to the edge of the hole.

My fingers and toes sharpened into shiny claws. My in-between state would have to do. I leaned over the pit. My scalp danced with the wild magic pouring from the aperture. Something more dangerous than an oversized snake lurked in that darkness.

I blinked at the blackness until I picked up a low, wavering light. My black sclera drank the shadows allowing my silver-ringed pupils to sift out shapes. The lower the sun dipped, the more details my eyes picked up.

Crumbling murals in native pigments stretched along curved walls. A cracked tile floor festooned with roots lay in muddy ruins below. The roughly football field-sized chamber inside the mound looked abandoned, but the smell alone told me it wasn't.

A whip of light cracked the sky, chased by a roll of deep-throated thunder. The flash blinded me for a moment and conjured a choir of sizzling hisses from the darkness below.

Definitely not abandoned.

I gripped the edge of the stone ring and leaned farther in.

Jump! The chaos inside me begged, but something about those roots on the floor felt wrong. A suffocating vision spun to life of me buried under a writhing pile of nagas as they all sank their fangs into me at once. The chaos at my center howled to be flung into that fray, but my higher reasoning pleaded for patience.

Chaos. Patience. Chaos. Patience. I weighed them both in my mind.

Guess which one won.

I quickly measured the length of the opening against my height and braced my hands and feet against the stones. If anyone other than snakes lurked below, they now had a great view up my dress. I'd worn my white undies with the little red hearts.

Cute and sexy.

What? A girl's gotta look good.

I clutched the spindly roots dangling from the chamber ceiling and tried to calculate a way to the floor that wouldn't involve a broken bone. My skeleton was way stronger than a human's but I wasn't indestructible.

Go, go! The chaos screamed like a banshee in my head. I inched down along the roots and rain-slick stones, but I hadn't balanced myself right. My left foot slipped out from under me and the shock of it loosened my tension against the stones. My legs fell and my hands tightened on the roots.

The roots ripped free.

Lightning flashed a circle of light on the muddy floor of the cavern. It glinted off the slick skin of the nagas waiting below.

I plummeted.

My back arched with muscle memory to catch the air with my wings, but my wings weren't there yet. They squirmed beneath my skin. Trapped until sunset.

I hit the slick floor feet first and slipped. My back took some of the force and then my head struck. A constellation of lights danced before my eyes.

You idiot.

I fought to my elbows. Chaos cheered in the back of my pounding head like I'd just scored a touchdown, but I hadn't. All I'd done was allow the mayhem inside me to choose my actions.

I wasn't stupid. I knew why the Council sent me on the most dangerous assignments. They hadn't sent me on this one, but they would have had they known about the naga presence in the Everglades.

No, I wasn't stupid, but I was rash and reckless and the

Council used me for it. One day, it would get me killed. I stuffed the bloom of bedlam deep down so that my brain might have a chance to assess the situation.

The shadows hissed at me. I hissed back. I stood and wiped the muck from my dress.

Gross.

My pupils spasmed as the owl in me fixed on the shapes darting through the faint light. Whispers echoed. I hunched my back and turned in a slow circle.

Thick, slithering bodies surrounded me.

As my eyes adjusted, I noticed that the Naga Loka held additional dimensions, similar to an Underhill. The central cavern had double the space that it took up in the human realm. A honeycomb of circular tunnels branched off in all directions. Some were filthy, rough-hewn holes burrowing away into blackness, while others were fairly clean and lined with brightly painted tiles.

The main chamber held the same contrasts. Vivid murals and boldly patterned tapestries decorated the crumbling walls. Floors with what appeared to be handmade tiles lay cracked and sinking. Every piece of this hidden kingdom was fading.

"Welcome," a sultry voice whispered through the dimness.

Something with its own gravity uncoiled in the shadows. I turned to the huge figure moving toward me in the darkness. It stopped just outside the circle of flashing storm light surrounding me.

"To what do I owe the pleasure, Little Fae?" The masculine voice dipped and rolled like the curves of a violin. He lingered on the word *pleasure* as if it were a pillow he'd just positioned beneath my hips.

"The Council requires all fae communities in North

America to register and submit to an inspection." My voice only shook a little.

"How interesting. If I am not fae—then what?" I'd never heard such an alluring voice before. The speaker's tone continued to rise and fall like a body in need of touching. His shadowy form moved closer until the pale storm light outlined his hulking features.

My breath caught.

The rounded mountain peaks of his shoulders and his smooth, hairless head slid into the light. Thick arms crossed like cannons over a chest the width of a wine cask. Twin gold wristbands separated his heavy forearms from fists the size of anvils.

I craned my neck to get a look at his face and that glint of amber glowing in the shadowed caverns of his eyes. A glistening, red whip flicked the air between us then vanished as quickly as it had appeared. I took a clumsy step back.

"All non-humans are required to—"

"How arrogant and assuming." The creature leaned over me, dragging the rest of his massive body into the light. Where legs would have been, a thick reptilian body bunched, stacking muscle upon rigid muscle. A ten-pack abdomen spread up his humanoid mid-section.

I gasped again as my gaze dropped to his lower half. At waist height his pale brown skin transitioned to a scale-like diamond pattern. Large, yellowish sections clustered at his midline giving way to smaller, iridescent versions running along his sides. As he swayed in the low light, I picked up a subtle pattern of dark bands ringing his trunk.

Something thick and heavy nestled among the segments of his lower abdomen. My heartbeat quickened forcing me to take a few deep breaths.

"How—human—of this Fae Council to present such an edict." His meaty serpentine tail coiled and thrashed behind him. "Have they not followed the political machinations of the humans? Have they not witnessed the rise and inevitable fall of the human dynasties, tyrants—councils?"

The sensual note in his voice sharpened to a syrupy sweet blade, serrated but still lickable. He lifted a segmented rattle high into the air. It teased the space around us, vibrating so quickly my eyes could barely register the movement. The manic motion mesmerized me. I shivered as a quivering energy danced along my skin.

Shadows hissed. The stagnant air thickened like a cock in my hand. The greedy pressure of the cavern rubbed against me from all angles.

"A congregation of fae, or any non-humans may destabilize the laws of nature and—"

"What do you know of nature's law, Little One?" Something in the way this massive creature said "Little" made my insides tingle. I was an average-sized female, but next to him, I felt small, almost fragile as if at any moment he might pick me up and place me on a shelf. A pretty treasure to play with when the mood struck. "Did you walk this planet when those rules were made?"

I backed to the far edge of the light and hit a wall. I hadn't seen a wall when I'd looked down into the cavern, but I felt it buzzing and solid against my back.

"I was," he whispered. The murmured words coiled around me.

Thunder rolled across the land, shaking the giant cave. The serpent-man's face drew close enough for me to see the curve of his shadowed brow. Eerie twin lights flashed from its depths. I followed the brutish bridge of his nose with my gaze down to his cruelly sensual mouth. His forked tongue teased the air again.

My heart set out at a jog as my lungs heaved the weighty air.

To a human, the bulging heap of his oversized muscles might appear monstrous. To a daughter of Eve, the curve of his fangs over his bottom lip may seem grotesque. I'd lived and worked with humans so long that I could recognize his visage as gruesome and yet my blood warmed at the thought of those savage hands reaching for me.

My pulse quickened again as I yearned for another glimpse of that bestial tongue.

He regarded me with those shrouded crescent moon eyes.

"I remember your foremother…the First Lilith. She was as beautiful as you."

My lungs shuddered to a stop, leaving my racing heart to struggle as I peered up at the giant half-man, half-snake hovering over me.

In the fae realms, Liliths were considered to be quite attractive. Because of that, hardly anyone paid us a compliment. Even so, a small morsel of praise like that shouldn't have felt so good…but it did.

His long, moist tongue flicked out of his fiendishly wide mouth and tickled across my jaw, then down my neck. My nipples tightened to straining peaks. That fluttering touch reached down through my chaos, straight to the trembling heart of my eros.

I pulled away.

"You smell like a Lilith. You taste like a Lilith, but you do not act like one."

"You don't quite fit the bill for a naga either," I quipped, reaching for my composure.

I'd seen big muscles before. I'd interacted with creatures this raw, this elemental, this enticing before, but that didn't stop my cerulean cheeks from flushing to a bright amethyst.

My thoughts turned to Hamus. That fiery moron with his impossibly thick biceps and tantalizing equipment hidden beneath his chainmail. My eyes dropped to the serpent-man's groin area.

Pull it together, Lil. He's just a big snake with a good workout regime…and a tongue made for more than licking… and a massive bulge in an anatomically perfect location.

I struggled to hide my heavy breathing.

A girl needs air, right?

"A naga?" The creature tilted his polished head back and laughed. The powerful sound shook me to my core. My gaze followed the cords of muscle roping his neck. They looked strong. Strong enough to sink my teeth into.

A flash of lightning, followed by a violent clap of thunder, cleared my thoughts a little. I'd lost control of this situation. This was supposed to have been a simple bag and tag. Find the naga. See if he has friends. Take a few samples somehow. Then, get back to my vacation already in progress.

The floor beneath my feet pulsed with energy as if that last bolt of electricity had given the chamber a heartbeat. The circle of sky above us strobed. Light glinted off the fierce tips of the serpent-man's fangs as his face drew uncomfortably close. Kiss-ably close. Lick-ably close.

What would it feel like to slip my tongue between those dangerously sharp points. Could I suck the burning venom from them? Would he like that?

"Look closer, Little Fae."

I leaned in and made the colossal mistake of looking the serpent in his sparkling, hypnotic, rapturous eyes.

11

THE IMMORTAL SERPENT

"ROOT OF ALL HUMAN EVIL"

Domain: Corporis
Kingdom: Unknown
Phylum: Eros
Class: Khaos
Order: Reptilia
Family: Serpentes
Genus: Unknown
Species: Unknown

Gilded orbs of liquid light held my gaze as my arms and legs grew heavy. The gleaming globes pulsed with the heartbeats of newborn stars. My eyes drank the golden glory until my body released every ounce of anxiety.

A deep and primal warning sounded in the back of my brain as my muscles relaxed.

I ignored it.

"Naga is an ancient Sanskrit word used to describe the

celestial serpents of the old world." The giant snake's tail slipped around my ankles. "Those magnificent creatures are long gone from this ever-changing land." The serpent-man's brows bunched for a moment, casting deep, sorrowful shadows over his glittering irises. The inky slits of his pupils swelled, parting the molten seas.

I blinked dazedly as if coming out of a glimmering dream, and then his pupils thinned. The hypnotic flickering of candlelight on golden treasure filled my mind again.

"The Nagas were only semi-divine."

His warm tail crept up my thighs.

The warning turned to a shrill shriek. I tuned it out. Instead, I let myself relish the warmth of his embrace. *When was the last time a man had wrapped himself around me?*

"When you use that term, you must be referring to my offspring." He waved a hand at the swaying shadows gathered around us. I tore my gaze from his long enough to take in the coiling of tails and flicking of tongues. "Yes, they are somewhat lacking. I am without a proper mate."

Their gimlet eyes twinkled in the low light.

Some reached for me with rudimentary fingers. Others flared their hoods in defense. A few of the larger ones slithered into the circle of storm-light with hunger riding their reptilian faces. Tension teased down the serpent-man's body and they backed away, but the fire of challenge flashed in their furtive gazes.

Maybe I smelled like food to them or maybe a different urge galvanized their attention. Hands reached low, brushing at thickening flesh on their undercarriages. My heartbeat quickened as their intentions became clear.

That's when I noticed it.

They possessed an anatomical difference that made me swallow hard. The nagas were using both hands to stroke their stiffening flesh. Their fists were clearly clamped onto two shafts each. Each male naga worked two cocks.

Some jerked their hands frantically as my gaze slid over them. Others calmly returned my heated stare while massaging their engorged columns. The slurp and slap of their moistened skin drummed through the darkness providing an erotic beat to their chorus of hissing.

My gaze darted to the serpent-man and the bulge below his waist. A thin seam between two of his segments strained to contain something sizeable.

His deep, syrupy chuckle poured over me.

"Do you see something you like, Little Girl?"

There it was again. *Little.* That word travelled through my body seeking places that needed cradling. I liked being called a girl too. Yes, I was a full-fledged woman, but there was also a small and very ignored part of me that was still a soft and dreamy, playful and curious little girl. That part of me wanted love too. It wanted to be touched, caressed, protected. Or, at the very least, seen.

The eros compulsion rose inside me like a tidal wave. My venereae nature flowed from the chaos at the core of my being. From the violence and hunger and cruelty of lust. It was as confused as I was by my reaction to this creature's words.

I'd learned to accept the rushed eruption of desire, the brutal frenzy of passion. I was a Lilith. Night Monster. Succubus. Murderous Lover. The Father Who Turned Away had made me like this. And as such, I was not meant to know affection. What I saw in the nagas' eyes was all I deserved. Mindless rutting.

Romance. Love. Tenderness. They weren't in the cards for me.

My thoughts floated to Daniel. Beautiful, kind, warm-hearted Daniel. I could never have him the way I wanted to.

Did he think I was beautiful too? Did he see the little girl inside me?

I glanced back at the serpent-man. The rattling tip of his tail probed beneath my dress. He'd pinned my legs closed, but he'd found the gap in my thighs. I gasped as the warm, wriggling end of him slithered over my heart-print undies.

"It's remarkable how much you resemble the Night Mother."

No creature, fae or any other, would dare touch my source of power so casually, and yet his delicious probing continued. His muscles tightened as he turned me in his grip to get a better look at my curves. His tongue flicked over my skin, my hair, my dress.

Eros flooded to every corner and crevasse of my being. The serpent breathed it in as if he were sampling the bouquet of a fine wine.

"When He banished Lilith from the Garden and replaced her with Eve…I wept."

I shook my head to try and clear my foggy thoughts. What had he just said about the Garden? Was he talking about the Garden of Eden?

His eyes swam with unshed tears.

"And here you are—a mirror image of her—brimming with carnal need."

His rattle twitched, slipping past my undies. Fiery pleasure curled through me as he slid the tip of his rattle along my slick cavern, brushing my opening and the bright, blooming peak just before it. I bucked and ground against the shivering vibration. My stomach fluttered.

"Please." The petals of my venereae anatomy swelled to welcome the plundering invader. The inflamed layers of my extra flesh lengthened, adding a little more depth to my vagina. My body was designed to accommodate all kinds of lovers—even partners as big as him. I'd had a few run-ins with oversized cocks, but I'd never really tested the limits of my one-size fits-all equipment.

No, I still won't show you. Just picture a rose but replace the petals with soft layers of swollen labia. Better yet—don't picture it at all.

I squirmed as the inflamed protrusions pushed against my clit. My silky moisture spread over his rattle and glistened down his tail. I'd never experienced the eros like this before. Where was the savagery? The barbarous incursion of lust?

"Be a good girl, Little Fae, and answer one question." He dragged his vibrating tail across my slick womanhood like a bow across the strings of a violin. I gasped.

My talons dug into his coils, but he didn't cry out. I brought the copper sweet drip of his blood to my lips. I licked the dark red liquid from my talon tip and the earth moved.

Gravity, heated particles, time and space crushed together to form everything we knew. The serpent's blood held dizzying designs, genetic blueprints—too many for my mind to comprehend. His flesh held the very map of life. All it needed was a spark to impregnate. The ember glow in his eyes was the fire of creation. He was the first. Before Adam.

The weight of that realization pressed down on me with a crushing force. Awe swept through me, clearing my head. What was the Great Tempter doing here in Florida, down a muddy hole in the Everglades? This was way more than I'd signed up for. I'd been chasing a simple reptilian reemergence, not the Immortal Serpent, one of the first creations of The Father Who Turned Away.

I twisted and wriggled in the grasp of his muscular coils as flight hormones cascaded through me, but it was too late —my body throbbed with need. I looked at the exit above me. My wings were only minutes away. I could feel it. But I was too far gone. I needed the serpent's touch more than I needed air to breathe.

"Tell me why you've really come?" The caressing tones returned to his voice.

The hulking creature drew me against him. Eros spilled from my hands as they flattened against his hard chest. He trembled. His warm flesh pressed against me as his great lungs filled with the fetid air.

Bodies thrashed around us. A chorus of hissing echoed through the cavern.

"I—I collect samples—for the Council—for its breeding program."

"Ah, breeding." His whiplash tongue probed my face, my lips. Its delicate, searching forks slipped into my mouth. I closed around the manic flickering strands of flesh and sucked. He tasted like the parts of the earth the sun never sees. The deepest soil. The darkest caves.

The snake-man groaned. His lantern eyes slid closed.

The rest of my missing awareness flooded back into my brain. I released his tongue and looked down at my body where it bumped and rubbed against his. My legs were pinned, but my arms were still free.

All around us serpentine bodies rolled and twined over the cracked tile floor. Slithering tails jerked as they coiled around one another. Fat, slippery cocks stretched toward glistening slits. Bodies spasmed as the turgid, seeking dual columns of flesh sank into quivering crevasses. No sooner had one rod of the nagas' hemi-penises buried into a wriggling female than it was withdrawn and the second glistening pillar sank home. Bodies bucked.

The coiling orgy set my flesh on fire.

"And will you be participating in this breeding program?" The towering serpent's silky voice grew husky and low.

His tail rubbed against my oiled flower with renewed

purpose. I cried out. I was free of his hypnotic eyes, but my body hung on his every trembling movement. I bloomed for him. My hips rocked, rubbing my tenderest parts against the buzzing chambers of his rattle as he dragged them against me.

"Answer me." His hot breath rolled down my neck.

"No, I will not," I moaned.

"But you are a pure strain of fae." He slipped the skinny straps of my sundress off my shoulders and down my arms. I didn't fight him.

I hadn't worn a bra. The sudden exposure sharpened my tips to aching points. His giant hands reached for me. Strong fingers trapped my straining pearls of pleasure as he cupped my soft mounds. "Why would they not want as many Daughters of the First Wife as possible?" His gilded eyes glittered.

"The curse." The answer slipped from my lips on a heaving sigh. My cheeks flushed with embarrassment and anger as I realized what he was doing to me. I'd slipped free of his mesmerizing eyes, but he'd entranced me with his touch.

His fingers rubbed together, dragging a moan from my lips. He rolled and pinched my nipples until he owned me. Until I ached with need.

"Yes—the curse," he whispered. "You may not keep a child until one hundred of your offspring have been devoured? That is a tragedy. Have you yet conceived? Are you steadily working your way through the curse, ripping away souls at the very start of their lives?"

His mouth curved cruelly. "I can only imagine what your poor mother must have endured to have you. One hundred murders. She must be quite mad by now." His grin stretched a little more.

"Do you have a close relationship with your mother,

Lilith?" My name slithered off his quivering tongue. The hot, cherry-red shame of my birth paraded across my face. I pushed his hands away.

No, I didn't have a relationship with my mother. I'd been her one and only birth. She'd traded her life for mine.

"You know…I could take that pain from you."

He gripped my waist where my dress had bunched. Beneath his anvil hands, heat rolled through me, melting the ever-present fae permafrost just beneath my skin. I reached for his fingers as they slid to my lower abdomen. A new, uncomfortable heat spread deep into my body. Desire tightened my muscles, but the burning grew more and more uncomfortable.

I gasped and tried to pull his hand away.

"I have a proposition for you." He lowered those glowing eyes to the level of my gaze, but I looked to the side. "You are just as He made your foremother, filled with life's potential." He moved his fingers and I felt a pinch in the side of my abdomen. "Do you want a child, Lilith?" His gaze seemed to see into my most hidden thoughts. "I can help you with that." His burning fingers slipped lower and another prick of pain stabbed my other side. "All you need do is give me one hundred plus one of your eggs to fertilize. I will…dispatch the first one hundred just as they hatch."

Hatch?

Some of my species could lay eggs, but I'd been a live birth. My mother had been a live birth. I had a normal mammalian female cycle.

Before you ask—no, my species is still none of your business.

I tried to fix on the meaning of his words, but his hand fought the clench of my thighs and his fingers searched the moistness his rattle had produced. My pulse raced as I pulled at his thick wrist, but his hand remained locked against me.

"I will keep the last for myself. Then, you will be free to mate and conceive as you please. The curse will be lifted."

Was that true? Could someone else play the role of executioner of my newborn children? If so, did that make any difference to my conscience? Would my decision not to harm infants change if I knew I had a real shot at a family of my own?

Then, my thoughts turned to the child he would keep for himself. A female child. My blood simmered.

The weight of his glittering stare pressed against me, but I kept my gaze focused on the chiseled curve of his cheek or the slant of his strong jaw. Had this handsome, terrifying creature been the prototype for Adam? And, more importantly, was he really offering me a way out of the curse?

"I—how?" I tried to form a question from the tangle of emotions roiling inside me, but my mind wouldn't produce words. His tail squeezed my legs as he turned my body to face away from him. He clutched my arm with one hammer-hard hand and used the other to bend me over. A chorus of hissing stirred to life around us.

"Allow me to show you."

12

BLOOD-BAT

"FLYING RAPTURE"

Domain: Corporis
Kingdom: Fae
Phylum: Thantos
Class: Khaos
Order: Sanguis (blood)
Family: Pteropods (winged feet)
Genus: Exsanguis (exsanguinator)
Species: Orgasmus Mordere (orgasmic bite)

I fought the urge to comply. It would feel so good to bend over and let someone else drive. Someone tall and strong and dangerous and…in control. I hated the surroundings, but loved being touched. The shifting muscles in his tail massaged my legs even as he held me tight.

I used the strength of the falling night to twist in his grip. My wings teased so close to the surface of my skin. My owl form begged for freedom.

"Be a good girl, Little Fae." The serpent tried to force me

back around. "Give me what I want, and I'll give you what you need." The calm authority in his voice weakened my resolve a little more. There was so much I wanted. So much I'd never had.

His coils squeezed. I strained against his grip.

"Do you want to be punished?" His masculine voice dipped deliciously low and that thick sense of gravity swelled between us.

The orgy went wild around us.

Daddy.

Fizzing fireworks burst in my stomach as the word drifted to the front of my thoughts.

Yes, Daddy. I wanted any sweet punishment he might give. Even if it hurt. Stung. Stole my breath.

I'd never even had a father. There'd been men who'd stepped in to help raise me, but I was a product of the system. My mother had mated with someone and chosen not to kill me at birth. So, I'd grown up in the Underhill with no real parents.

Had this ancient creature just woken something inside me? How could I have a Daddy Kink if I'd never had a daddy to begin with?

Oh, don't act so shocked. You have a kink too. You just haven't met the right monster yet.

The snake-man's formidable presence hung over me. Iridescent scales flashed along the sides of his muscular abdomen. Black rings stretched and bunched along his tail as he stacked his coils around me. His age pressed against my body like a giant paperweight.

The Immortal Serpent, the destroyer of The Garden of Eden, was likely the father of many lines of life forms. He was, in many ways, the ultimate Daddy. Just thinking about it turned the pyrotechnics in my stomach into a full-blown centennial celebration.

I wanted to be someone's Little Girl…someone's Good Girl. But I was a night monster. A fiend with an overactive sex drive. Good girls were delicate humans with pigtails and too many curves spilling from beneath their babydoll nighties.

I wasn't a good girl. I ate good girls for breakfast. And yet…I trembled with the need to say the word out loud.

Daddy.

I wanted to be told what to do, and rewarded with praise if I followed instructions. I wanted stolen touches from someone who would caress me for being good or spank me for being bad. But even as I thought it, I knew this wasn't the creature to dominate me in that way. An image of Hamus flashed before my eyes and anger burned through me. That was a white-hot thread I didn't want to pull on right then.

I wrestled in his grip until I faced the giant serpent again.

"Maybe we can come to an arrangement," I purred and reached for the bulge between the plates of his segments. His thick, winding body bowed to accommodate me.

Eros poured from my hands as I rubbed his straining flesh. A spasm shook the serpent's entire body as the first of his thick, luscious cocks sprang free. The massive column reminded me of a cactus, but its spines looked soft and flexible. My insides shuddered at the thought of those filaments prodding my soft tunnel. I'd never had a lover with two cocks before. My brain heated with possibilities.

"This is my kingdom. You will do as I say, Little One." His words had grown breathy and halting.

Oh, I intended to, but first there was a smidge of business to tend to.

"I'm very tempted by your offer to free me of my curse, but…may I have time to think about it?" I risked a glance at his mesmerizing eyes. I saw pleasure and fury, disappointment and plans. So many plans.

The monstrous snake-man leaned over me until his avalanche of muscle threatened to crush me.

"This is a one-time offer, I'm afraid." His eyes burned like lanterns on the darkest of nights. I kept my gaze lowered.

"Oh, really?" I coaxed his second member from its hiding place. With a soft brush of my fingers, it swelled into a long smooth column with a crown of soft pink flesh, similar to a flower, at its tip. The strange appendage piqued my interest and tightened my insides.

"You do not know what you are walking away from," he hissed, but I could tell he was trapped by the snare of our desire as much as I was. His words lacked force.

"Even if you could harvest my eggs, I can't allow any of my potential children to be harmed. But, as I said—" I ran my hands down each of his stiffened columns and he bucked and shook with burning need. "—I thank you for the offer."

Is it awful to admit that I regretted my words as soon as I'd said them?

"Surely you must know I will take what I want with or without your consent." The Immortal Serpent's true colors finally made an appearance. He really was a greedy, self-serving, egocentric malcontent. But I didn't need him to be a good guy. I didn't need him to be my daddy. I needed him to finish what he'd started.

Somewhere far away, across the ocean, the sun's last rays slipped below the horizon. Night drew its starry blanket over me, and its moonlight fingers brushed against me as gently as a mother's touch. Two soft, downy wings sprang from my back, powerful and damn near indestructible. My talons stretched. My eyes widened. My muscles tightened, pulsing with strength.

I gave the biblical brute gripping me a feral smile. "You can take your pleasure, but you won't be taking anything else." My venereae eros flooded over him like a tidal wave. It filled the cavern, drowning the nagas in mindless need. "Don't worry. I'll be gentle."

The serpent's coils went limp as I forced the first of his cocks into my mouth and nursed it with my tongue.

He cried out in what sounded like shock.

I slid the swollen missile as far in as my jaw would allow. Then, I dragged it out and pushed it in again. My lips strained. My tongue teased the tiny spine-like tendrils.

The serpent moaned. The deep sound rolled like the thunder outside. I ran my hand over his second cock, feeling its length, caressing the bloom of flesh at its tip. His lanterns extinguished as his eyes slid closed.

I gripped his first cock with both hands and worked the shaft until the serpent's breath quickened. Then, I leaned over and rolled my tongue over the bright crown of flesh on his other pillar. A groan rolled up from deep in his chest.

I took the smooth rod in my mouth and bobbed my head as I swallowed it down. The serpent gasped.

I experimented with each column until I found a rhythm of sucking and stroking both monstrous appendages. I marveled at their differences. Each cock seemed built for varying stimuli. The serpent groaned with pleasure if I jerked the base of his spiny cock while sucking its head. His coils quaked if I licked the bloom of his smooth cock while slowly stroking its shaft. I still didn't know what that extra bit of brightly-colored anatomy was for, but I was excited to find out.

Venereae eros dribbled over us like intoxicating syrup.

His body undulated as I sucked and jerked his cocks until they were slippery with pre-seed. Then, I eased my mouth off and lightened my touch.

"You will collect blood and tissue samples from your nagas and the humans outside and have them sent to the laboratory for Functional Anatomy and Evolution at Hans Jodkins University.

His guttering lanterns blazed bright.

"You do not give orders to The Immortal Serpent," he roared, and the orgy shuddered to a stop.

He studied me so closely I thought I could feel him rummaging around in my head.

"Daddy gives the orders."

I shivered as those words sank deep. I wanted to play this new game, but I wasn't ready to hand over my power. Not yet.

"If you do this, I will forget that I met you and only report on an infestation of reemergent naga hybrids."

I let go of his twin columns and leaned back into his loose coils. I nestled in the thick ropes of warmth and let a little more of my eros sink into his skin. The remains of my sundress rode high on my thighs. I lifted one leg and draped it over a coil.

The air roiled around his ancient body as he seethed. He struggled against my eros, but there was no use. He might have been one of the first creatures to walk this earthly plane, but he was still burdened with the same needs and drives as the rest of us. He couldn't escape my particular brand of enchantment.

The moist edge of my heart-print undies peeked from beneath the thin material of my dress.

The serpent's tongue flicked the air like a bright red pennant.

I caressed the loops of his long body, and he responded, rolling against me, cradling my soft wings, nudging my legs farther apart.

"What will you give me for my cooperation, Little Fae?" He folded at the waist bringing his massive face to hover just above me. The forks of his tongue brushed my lips, the curve of my jaw, the tender skin of my neck.

"What would you like?"

I reached for his bestial face. My fingers slipped along his curved mouth. I dragged a fingertip down the length of one fang. The snake-man's eyes closed again as if savoring my touch.

"It has been eons since I've enjoyed a Lilith's attentions." His eyes opened just a hint. "Ages since I've tasted a Lilith's bloom." His face dipped to my skirt as he breathed in my scent. "And your cravings are so…unique."

I gave him a questioning look.

"A succubus who wants to be a Good Girl—very unusual. Almost undeniable."

"I'm not a good girl."

"Aren't you?"

"Aren't you everything a daddy wants in a good little girl?"

Those words set my brain on fire.

His tongue flicked my thighs so lightly, it felt just like the supple flutter of a blood-bat's wings. I'd only been bitten once by a blood-bat and it had been the most erotic sensation of my life. The cave-dwelling creature's toxins produced a prolonged orgasm to distract its prey while it feed. So far it held the trophy for best climax, but that was before I'd experienced a giant serpent's tongue. Things were looking up.

"Let me please you," he stated more than asked. His rattle freed itself from the tangle of coils and slithered between my legs. Blood rushed to all the right places. My breath quickened.

I held my hand up to ward off the tantalizing tip.

"Only if you promise not to relieve me of any of my eggs."

I was beginning to guess at the purpose of his extra

appendage—the one with the fleshy pink crown. His rattle shook with what looked like agitation.

"A taste is all I will take."

With that, he reached for my skirt with his bulky humanoid hands. I leaned back as he pushed the hem up over my hips. Hot breath spilled over my undies. I squirmed.

"Such a sweet elixir," he whispered and tore my cutest pair of panties from my body.

This better be good, I thought, *or he owes me a gift card to Victoria's Closet.*

13

GOOD GIRL

"DADDY'S LITTLE TOY"

Domain: Corporis
Kingdom: Fae
Phylum: Eros
Class: Ordo
Order: Submissive
Family: Little Vixens
Genus: Naughty and needs to be spanked
Species: Does what Daddy says

I *think we've established that I've had my fair share of sex. Right?*

Keep in mind that there are fae that have lived centuries longer and bumped uglies with more creatures than can be counted. With that said, I'd not encountered any that could manipulate gravity and space to the point that they could levitate their lover's body.

Until now.

The Immortal Serpent's coils quivered with a primordial

energy that should have been buried deep at the planet's core or tucked away in the heavens for baffled physicists to discover. How this magical being had come to be holed up in a mountain of mud on a flood plain barely high enough above sea level to be called land was a story for another time, I guessed.

The trembling vibration thrilled through me draining my legs of weight. Hollowing out my midsection. I folded my wings against my back as I left the warm cradle of his coils. I wanted to giggle at the lightness but that would have been unbecoming of a Lilith. Nevertheless, the little girl inside me quietly tittered with glee as I began to float.

My head hung as if from a cloud as his tongue flitted down my inner thighs. The forked points whispered along my skin. The manic, flickering ribbons of heated flesh dove deep into the bend where my thighs ended and my garden began. Then, vanished without warning.

"Be good for Daddy and spread your legs," he growled.

My heart pounded against its cage as the gentle, yet stern command spread like gasoline through my veins. I squirmed for a moment inside the new parameters he'd set, and then I quickly complied. I spread my thighs wider.

"What do you say when Daddy gives you an instruction?"

Fuck off?

Kiss my Lilith-blue ass?

Go to the Wells?

Deadly Lilith energy raged inside me. I wasn't Thantos by nature, but if this creature had even a drop less power, my sudden fury might have torn him into a million pieces. But, slowly, and with a tickling surrender, I let the little girl in me answer.

"Yes, Daddy," I whispered. That single act of submission doused the flames of my outrage. The embers of my indignation hissed and cooled. In reward, his tongue pressed and probed anew. It danced so close to my aching split, I whimpered. I relished the teasing touch until the pulse in my core screamed for attention.

A wave of eros swelled over me. The chorus of hissing around us turned to strangled screeching.

A sigh escaped my lips as his glistening twin tongue-tips raced over my slick cavern, danced on my rising peak for one searing bright moment, then skittered down to my tunnel and the swollen flower at its gate.

"So sweet. Like warm honeysuckle on the vine." He lapped at my folds and tickled over my stiffening bud. "Such a good little fae."

I gasped and squirmed and tilted my hips as his tongue delved deep into my crevice. His words plunged deeper. He slid the tender tips of his tongue inside me, dragged them out, then drove them in again. I moaned and squirmed as he spread my legs wider.

His tongue recoiled into his mouth as he tasted my essence and went back for more. But, even as the tickling tines plundered my most vulnerable parts, his long, hard fangs pressed into the soft flesh of my thighs.

With barely a thought, he could rake me with his venomous tips. He could plunge those sharpened points straight into an artery and his undiluted toxins, formed when the world was new, would burn through my veins, searing muscles, collapsing capillaries.

Would I survive a bite from the Immortal Serpent himself? The chaos inside me yearned to roll that dice.

I bucked with pleasure as the wider part of his tongue dragged over my turgid nub. Fear should have snapped me out of the sex haze, but the razor-sharp certainty that I might die before reaching release drove me to a new height of arousal. I wriggled with the desire to ride his long fangs and see where it took me.

"Daddy wants you to hold still now."

I wrestled with the knee-jerk response to tell him to go to hell. Then, I fought to calm my movements. My body stilled.

"What do you say when Daddy tells you what to do."

Butterflies. Sparking, flaming, exploding butterflies.

"Yes...Daddy."

"Good girl."

I quivered with pleasure. He pressed his palms into my thighs holding them as wide as they'd go. His rattle shook the air just above my hungry flesh. The delectable quaver trembled oh-so-close to my tiny summit.

I barely had time to take a breath before he plunged his buzzing tail into my Lilith bloom and my world caught fire. I rolled my hips and cried out as the rattle stayed with me, plundering my blossom, forcing its way deeper and deeper.

"Yes," I screamed. Eros erupted from me like a geyser.

His tongue points found my sacred mound again and trapped it between the two rubbing prongs. I writhed and rolled as the pinching, squirming tendrils massaged me to a feverish peak. I rode the pillow of air he'd created while his tongue and rattle worked my dripping seat of power. Even if I wanted to break free of his achingly delicious ministrations, there was no escape. He'd wrapped his tail around my wrists and clamped his powerful hands on my ankles.

My venereae parts sucked at his vibrating tail ravaging the quaking rattle, but it wasn't the piece of him it wanted.

"I want you to take me from behind." I begged in a small voice. A soft, pleading voice that couldn't be mine.

"I want you to take me from behind...what?" His dripping tongue slicked along his grinning mouth.

"I want you...to take me...from behind...Daddy."

His tongue returned to my burning flesh for one bright, fizzing moment and then recoiled.

"Good girls get what they want only after they've done what Daddy says."

The words were kindling in my belly.

He had me.

At that moment, the serpent between my legs could have asked me to do anything and I would have. Where had the night monster gone? I was Lilith. The Killing Pleasure. This game was in direct conflict with my very being. And yet I'd relinquished control. I'd submitted to this infuriating, delectable creature.

"Give me what I want, and I'll let you live." I tried to regain a bit of my power, but my words drained of danger.

His tongue returned to my feverish flesh. His rattle invaded my throne of strength, forcing me to new heights of rapture.

My legs quaked.

My stomach muscles tensed.

I raced up the hill of ecstasy at breakneck speed.

"Not until you release for Daddy. Be a good girl and do as I say." He buried his flesh deep in my garden. "Say it."

The tips of his fangs grazed either side of my burning slit, leaving sizzling trails. The pain sharpened my pleasure to a scorching, blistering, fiery point. I danced against his perilous mouth. He lapped me hard and fast. I moaned and rocked with the rhythm as I crested the summit.

"Say it."

My body spasmed on the cushion of air as my venereae eros burst from me in all directions.

"Yes, Daddy!"

His tongue thrust once, twice, and I exploded over and over. Every nerve in my body lit with pleasure. The power of creation washed through me. I quivered on the cradle of air as my body released years of hidden cravings, half-realized desires, denied dreams.

Is this what my previous lovers had felt when I'd dominated them? Did everyone have a special kink or fetish buried deep inside them? Were there more inside me?

I drifted down like a feather as mirky questions swirled through the euphoria in my head. I'd never experienced such pure rapture. Maybe the Liliths of old had known sexual bliss like that, but clearly I paled in comparison. I was a Lilith in a bottle. Contained. Pressurized. Stifled.

The serpent settled my quaking body back on the nest of his coils. His life force flickered all around me, but it didn't feel like I'd absorbed any of it.

I hadn't even formed a complete thought when his brutish hands grabbed me again and turned me over. I sprawled, weak as a baby against his coils.

"Now, you will do as I say." The serpent bent me over the wall of his looping tail and pinned me in place with one giant hand. "You've been a bad girl."

He lifted my dress to reveal my supple, heart-shaped ass. "Do you know what bad girls who barge into my domain making demands get?"

My chest fluttered with anticipation.

"Bad girls get fucked."

"Hard."

14

LILITH/NAGA FERTILIZATION

"LITTLE POSSIBILITY"

Domain: Corporis
Kingdom: Fae
Phylum: Oh, Goddess
Class: I can't be
Order: There's no way
Family: Fuck
Genus: I think, maybe
Species: I'm pregnant

I barely had time to brace before his thick, spiny cock pressed at my opening. He pushed through the soaked petals of my venereae blossom. I cried out, writhing in the sweet mix of pleasure and pain. He gave a quick, shallow shove into my sucking tunnel. My flesh burned and stretched to its limit.

This might not work. A sinking fear pooled in my stomach. *He's not going to fit.* I clambered over his coils to try and get some distance from his over-sized flesh torpedo.

"Oh, no." He grabbed me by my waist and dragged me back. I flared my wings in defense, but he clutched my hips tighter. "Bad girls take it all."

He pushed into me again, but this time he didn't stop.

I clenched my teeth together and held my breath as he filled me all the way to my end. I hung from his rocky pillar as he dragged it out and thrust it in again. My clawed feet left the floor. I was at his mercy.

"You can cry if you want to, but you have to take it like a big girl." He rammed into me again and my body clenched. I felt another pinch in my side.

The serpent withdrew and I turned to see him grab his other rod. He directed the smooth column with the gorged crown of bright pink flesh toward my slippery grotto.

"No." I scratched and scrambled my way to the top of the nest he'd made for me. I twisted to face him with my claws extended toward his face. "Not that one."

I wasn't sure what the particular bit of anatomy was for, but I had a feeling I didn't want any part of it.

He regarded me for a long, silent moment. He seemed to be thinking something over. His hands slid slowly over both his cocks as he gazed at me with something that looked similar to respect.

"As you wish, Little Fae. Bend over and we will find another place for it."

My legs went weak.

I'd had lovers with unusual bodies before, but this…this might be too much even for a Lilith.

Fight or flight paralyzed me half way between both. At that moment, he could have shoved me over and taken me any way he wanted. Instead, he leaned over me and whispered, "Daddy says bend over." His low, gravelly tone filled with warning, but he didn't touch me. He waited.

I met his candlelight gaze defiantly, but as I stared him down, I felt my body turning. I leaned back over his coils.

"Be a good girl and put your rump in the air."

"Yes, Daddy." A brushfire rushed through my veins as I barely whispered the words. I dipped my spine and presented my backside.

"Good girl." His words rolled through me. White hot pressure built between my legs again. I shivered as the tendrils of his enormous cock tickled against me. I leaned into him with dripping anticipation.

"Do you want it, Baby Girl?" the giant snake-man whispered. He caressed my hair.

"Yes."

"Will you take it all without complaining?"

"Yes."

"Yes, what?"

"Yes...Daddy." Tears of pleasure pooled in my eyes.

He leaned forward and pressed that oiled cannon into me slowly. Calmly and with skilled attention, he pushed and pulled it in and out stealing a little more depth with each thrust. Spines tickled and dragged, catching my juices and spreading them over his plundering shaft.

I moaned and gripped his coils as my muscles relaxed for him.

His hips rolled as he found the closest thing to a rhythm he could manage with such a tight fit. Each thrust shoved me into his heated coils like a bully on a human playground.

I took it without complaint, but I couldn't help but whine as each thrust filled me completely.

Just when I'd assumed he'd given up on finding a new place for his second, thinner cock, I felt a pressure at the puckered bud of my exit door. The delicious tapping synchronized with his thrusts until the mesmerizing sensation relaxed my tightened knot.

I strained to look over my shoulder and was confused to see his right hand stroking his other cock in time with his thrusts. My gaze dropped to his other hand which was lost in the curves of my ample cheeks.

The finger taps became small invasions that held my aperture open for long wriggling moments. The small incursions swelled my desire until I yearned for another raider. A twin torpedo of ramming pleasure.

"Take a deep breath, Little One," the Immortal Serpent whispered close to my ear. The gravity of his mass and his words pressed against me.

I sucked in the heavy air and tried to relax my bottom. Between two thrusts of his enormous cock, a new invader breached my body. I fought to stay relaxed as an aching pressure forced my body wide. He'd stuffed his slimmer cock half way into my other opening and was using the dribbling elixir coating my thighs to slide back out and in again.

"Just relax."

I gripped his coils and screamed to the rapturous night. I shouted to the heavens as the serpent took me in a staggered rhythm that stole the strength from my limbs. I hung onto the loops of his tail as he gripped my breasts. He trapped my aching tips between his fingers and crushed my back against his giant chest.

A sharp hissing sliced the air above me as his body began to shake.

I hung from his grasp as he pillaged me from behind. I rocked and slid and bucked as I rode that warm swell inside me back to its peak.

We rode it together.

My venereae flower tightened around his spiny cock and sucked it with each of his thrusts.

He cried out and gripped my hips with shaking hands. My body nursed his pre-seed, dragging tendrils of his life-force with it. The serpent grunted as if he'd completely lost the power of speech. Energy gathered as slithering shadows swarmed around us.

I reached a hand out to hold the nagas off, but my fingers hit another wall. The Immortal Serpent must have erected some sort of invisible field to hold them off. With that sense of safety, I leaned into my lover and gave myself to our dance.

He spanked me with his body as he rammed into me over and over. He gave a quivering shove and then another. The next quaking thrust pushed me over the edge and a tidal wave of eros washed through the cavern. Or, at least it seemed to. We were caught in a maelstrom of our own passion.

He erupted inside me like a volcano.

Eros crashed against the protective shield and washed back over us.

His seed, heavy with the designs of the universe, flooded through me. His fluids overflowed, spilling uselessly down my thighs. Even in my state of complete euphoria, I thought of the tests we could run on his sperm. I tried to imagine what wonders waited in his genes. But I'd assured the Immortal Serpent that I would keep his existence a secret.

His nagas were another story. They carried his genetic material, mixed—from the looks of it—with human blood.

I was barely able to accommodate him as a lover with my special adaptations. I couldn't imagine how he'd managed to mate with humans. I was clearly missing a lot of information.

He slid his twin appendages from my body and I collapsed against his warm tail. My body buzzed with his raw, elemental life force. I'd never felt so weak and yet so filled with strength.

"You are worthy of your name, Lilith." The snake-man's masculine voice rumbled with satisfaction.

He shifted, unwinding his coils, until I found myself unceremoniously deposited onto the dirty floor. The serpent slithered out of the faint pool of twilight into the deepest shadows of the cavern.

I glanced around at the furtive movements of the smaller serpents. Something scraped the floor near my feet. I turned just in time to see a snake with an almost human face and two strong arms push something heavy toward me.

I stood just as the pain stabbed my head. It knocked me back on my heels. My vision blurred. For the second time in a day, I'd been sucker punched by wild energy. I blinked at the serpent as it backed away from the stone it had just deposited.

I stumbled toward it, gripping my head. A blazing symbol glowed from the carved channels in the stone. I knew that marking. It was the sign for Eve.

Dread washed away the last of my post-coital euphoria as I reached my hand in the direction the Immortal Serpent had gone. My fingers hit another buzzing, invisible wall.

I looked around me until I found the two other stones in the darkness. Their symbols flared to life. One held the fiery sigil for Adam and the other sign glowed in the shape of the Immortal Serpent.

That bastard had trapped me.

I was in a trine.

15

HIMALAYAN CAVE NAGA

"CELESTIAL SERPENT"

Domain: Corporis/Incorporis
Kingdom: Human
Phylum: Eros
Class: Ordo
Order: Reptilia
Family: Serpentes
Genus: Nagini Supernal (female oracle naga)
Species: Until we know for sure she isn't fae, let's just leave this blank.

You've heard of feng shui—the spatial arranging of human stuff to alter the flow of energy around more human stuff, right? No? That's not how you define it?

Regardless of whether that definition is correct, understanding how a trine works requires you to understand how energy flows. We don't have time for that lecture, so I'll just say a trine is like moving your furniture around in your living room so that it surrounds your husband's recliner and traps him. The barriers are made of energy which can't be destroyed, only transformed or redirected. So basically, he can never leave. He might be okay with that, but unless someone disrupts the trine from the outside—he's staying put.

There are natural trines and intentionally manufactured trines. It's very hard to dismantle a handmade trap from the inside. And impossible if the trine is tailored for someone specific. As a direct descendant of the First Wife, this one was definitely made for me.

I'd underestimated the Immortal Serpent.

With every painful pulse of the deadly triangle, my strength leached from my body. My cellular bonds buzzed and vibrated until my skin itched. It was as if a giant had inserted a straw into my chest and now sucked my life force like a Lilith smoothie.

Even as chaos howled inside me, I knew I was running out of time.

Could I outthink an entity as old as creation?

I sank to my knees. Weakness gnawed at my muscles. I struggled to stay focused as my thoughts grew fuzzy and indistinct.

"Attacking a field agent is a direct affront to the Fae Council of Elders."

"I have not assaulted you."

My captor motioned to the nagas that still stood. They slithered over the limp forms of their fallen comrades and began to lick the serpent's body clean.

I took in the devastation around me. More than half the hybrid creatures in the cavern were now sprawled across each other in twisted clumps of lifeless flesh. Mouths gaped. Eyes stared into oblivion.

Off in a deeper pocket of shadows, I thought I glimpsed a quiver of movement. Maybe they weren't all dead.

I dropped to my palms next to the stone with the

glowing figure of a pregnant fertility goddess. The two circles of Eve's breasts, each surrounding a small glowing dot, conjured the power of life, nourishment, and motherhood. The fecund triangle of her genitals called to the exaggerated rod of Adam's radiating penis.

She was everything I was not.

"You are my guest," he sneered.

"Prisoner," I whispered to the broken tiles beneath me.

"Vessel," he offered as he drew close. His lantern eyes flickered in his swaying head. His massive body coiled and knotted on the other side of the barrier. "I was prepared to lift your curse, Little Fae. This could have been a mutually beneficial transaction."

"And now, what is it?"

My stomach lurched as the warped energy crackled around me.

"It is an exchange." The rich, masculine tones of his voice had lost their allure. "You will give me the fertilized egg inside you, and I will give you your freedom."

Oh, Goddess.

Fertilized egg?

My mouth went dry.

My gaze settled on the glowing circle depicting Eve's pregnant belly.

I'd been careless with other lovers, but nothing had ever come of it. I'd never been pregnant before. I'd thought maybe it was harder for Liliths to get with child…because of the curse…because The Father Who Turned Away had deemed us unworthy of new life.

My eye caught another quiver of movement close to my enclosure. A narrow-chested female with green and blue scales struggled beneath a pile of larger, immobile males. I focused on her in an attempt to avoid the meaning of the words he'd just uttered. Her giant irises glittered in the low light as she studied my face from her pinned position.

"This won't hurt…much," my captor taunted.

I dragged my gaze back to the hulking figure of the undying serpent. He seemed invigorated as he stared at me through the warping wall of energy.

He slowly stroked his long, smooth cock back to life. Its fuchsia crown of flesh swelled to full bloom.

I flexed my wings and tried desperately to create a box in my head for the blinding pain. My pale blue flesh practically glowed with the energy I'd syphoned from him, but it didn't matter. I couldn't wield it in this condition. Eventually, the trine would steal it all, transform it, and return it to its original owner. He had me.

"I'm not going down without a fight," I whispered weakly.

My head drooped.

"Oh, I think you will."

My limbs shook as if I'd been in the Wells with the Soul Seepers.

That stray mental image steered my thoughts back to the Underhill. To the good and the bad in my life. To Daphne and Daniel and all my friends—fae and human alike. Once the Immortal Serpent was done with me, he'd kill me or imprison me. Either way, I'd never see them again. I'd never see…Hamus.

Flames licked to life inside my mind, accompanied by that strange mix of loathing and white-hot desire. The flickering fire merged into two giant dragon wings. Then, from the stilted patchwork of my memory, strong arms reached from the charcoal shadows. Molten chainmail and granite muscle dripped and cooled like hardening magma.

He turned.

His glowing gaze found me across space and untold

dimensions. It felt as if the fire demon was peering through the mud and roots and rocks of my prison, past the wavering energy field of the trine, and into my shuddering soul.

"Lilith." My name whispered from his lips like steam. His ancient eyes widened with shock.

"Hamus?" I stared at the gloom above me. Had I called to him? I'd never called to an Old Order fae before. Besides my little accident with Domov, I'd never called to anyone. I wasn't strong enough for that. Was I? Domov was a fae-in-thrall. He could be called by anyone stupid enough to use his full name.

A ghostly heat warmed my skin.

What was happening? Was this far-seeing? I'd heard of the talent to remote view but it was rare. Only fae with a ton of mana could communicate mentally over great distances. Was Hamus that powerful?

There was one other way to far-see, but that was only between mated fae in the most dire of circumstances.

The heat on my skin grew uncomfortably warm. I braced for the impact of his famed temper, but it didn't hit. Hamus wasn't in the cavern with me. Yet, his presence wrapped around me like fierce, claw-tipped wings.

"You are near death." The draco-daemon's voice echoed through my skull. His words weren't so much sounds as colors and emotions. It was as if I could feel his shock cooling to something blue and sad…remorse. I scooped that sorrowful color into my hands and it warmed and softened into an orange acceptance tinged with the pale yellow of hope.

"Tell me where you are. I will send help." The colors liquified to dripping desperation.

"I think it's too late." My head touched the muddy floor. I surrendered to the pain. The trine drank the last of my energy.

The grimy ink of his anger blackened the edges of his ember-bright image. That was the way I would remember Hamus—angry and full of hate. I lost sight of him as my eyelids grew heavy.

The snake-man slithered close.

I spared a glance at the small female naga crushed beneath the bodies of her brethren. Her desperate expression reflected our circumstances perfectly. Everything had boiled down to this aching moment. I could barely believe my joyous trip to Florida to relax and regain the lost pieces of myself had been leading here—to this dark place, among these wretched creatures.

The delicate naga's eyes shimmered like wrinkled gold foil. Her iridescent skin stood out against the darker coils of the nagas draped over her. If not for the mud and angry abrasions, she might have been considered beautiful. Fragile.

She was definitely as out of place as I was. We'd both stumbled into a nightmare, and now, we would meet our ends together. It was comforting in a way.

"Pleassssse," she hissed with a breath it seemed she'd been hanging onto for dear life.

The giant man-serpent dipped close so that I would see his gloating grin. I took in his malignant pleasure, and I also caught the furtive movement below his notice. The little female had freed one arm and stretched it dangerously close to the serpent. Her fingers gripped the nearest stone. Her thin palm covered Eve's sigil, blocking out half the symbol. The stone went dark.

The pain in my head left me so quickly you'd think I'd just had a chiropractic adjustment. Energy hung in the air like the liquid from a burst bubble—a sloppy, steamy sex bubble. That energy was mine and it returned to me, slipping through my pores, converting to instant mana. It felt like I'd just gobbled a thousand pixies at once.

Strength poured through me.

The serpent's lantern eyes focused on the darkened stone.

"What have you done?"

He reached down and fastened an anvil hand on the naga's wrist. She cried out as he dragged her free of the knotted flesh piled on top of her. The stone flared anew completing the tailor-made trine once more, but I was no longer in it. My silent wings had carried me away.

True night descended on the Everglades awakening all the nocturns, stirring the manic, night-eyed insects. Predators roamed the hummocks and winding waterways.

The Night Mother's breath blew softly over the entrance to the Naga Loka. I clung to the edge of the stone ring and breathed the fresh air. The storm had passed, leaving only starlight and clean ocean breezes. It would have been so easy to have launched into the air and flown far away from that cursed place. But that was not what I did.

Maybe you might have. Maybe The Father Who Turned Away might have overlooked a cruelty like that, the way he overlooks so much that humans do. But I made a different choice.

I dove deep into the fetid cave, through the tangled roots, past the snarls of dead and dying bodies and perched on the shoulders of the Deceiver. My talons dug deep, ripping at skin and slicing muscle.

He dropped the female naga and reached for me, but I'd already settled at his ear. I whispered to him of tantalizing touches and sultry sucks. I promised him languid licks and ripe, red, ravishing release.

He fought to gain control, but I had him by his limbic system. My venomous seduction sank deep into his marrow. The ancient monster, the tempter, the cause of all human evil sank to the floor beneath my grip.

I'd used my Lilith eros to bring down big prey before. I'd seduced more genetic samples than I could count. But the power I'd consumed from that primordial creature had increased my strength by a magnitude I could not yet fathom.

"Had you given me more time to think about it, I might have taken you up on your offer." It was my turn to taunt him.

I left the overgrown snake to writhe on the floor, locked in a rapture without release.

I gripped the blue-green female in my talons and left that dirty, forgotten place. I flew into the glittering darkness.

Into the Night Mother's arms.

16

THRESHOLD SURFER

"SKIMBOARD HOTTIE"

Domain: Corporis
Kingdom: Human
Phylum: Eros
Class: Ordo
Order: Aperculum/Primate
Family: Intervallum/Hominidae
Genus: Homo
Species: Sexy Sapien

As the day drifted by, I made sure to work a little red into the faint tan of my glamour. It looked healthy and more like what people would expect from someone that had been in the sun all day.

Dalia drifted toward me along the beach from the general direction of the bar. She had two umbrella-topped coconuts in her hands. She'd talked Jim into holding down the fort while we took a long weekend in the Keys. She'd claimed her nerves needed it after the birthday debacle, but as we'd peeled away from the house in her soccer mom van, the sound of our conspiratorial laughter could have been heard for blocks.

In all honesty, I was a little worse for the wear. Losing my cell phone and credit card somehow wasn't as bad as losing my favorite sandals. Thank Goddess, I'd left my travel Visa and Identification Card at the hotel. Replacing those would have been harder than arranging the shipping for a live naga back to the Maryland Underhill.

My new naga friend had agreed to the terms of our breeding program in exchange for her eventual return to her home country of Tibet.

I was hoping she'd stay a while. I liked her. We'd thought the celestial nagas of the Himalayas were extinct. We'd already learned so much about her breed, like the fact that female celestial nagas could see the future. Maybe we could persuade her to stay beyond the terms of her agreement. Having an oracle on staff would be handy. It might stop me from blundering into trines or jumping down snake-infested holes.

Sex with the giant serpent-man had been costly too. Human pregnancy tests wouldn't work on me. At least, not yet. If I was with child, my bosses might be annoyed at losing their best field agent, but if my baby was female, they'd have a replacement Lilith in a few years. It was the only choice. I would never be able to kill my own child. I'd decided—if I was pregnant, I'd surrender my life to the curse. Maybe, one day, there would be a better option for my daughter.

That dark thought didn't fit with my beautiful surroundings.

"I know you don't like those plastic cups so I asked the bartender to make our drinks in these." She handed me a coconut. She was still the most fae-friendly human I'd ever met.

Dalia flopped into the beach chair next to me and we sipped our drinks.

Waves crashed.

Seagulls circled in the afternoon sun.

The salty breeze forced me to take a deep breath and push my potential pregnancy and likely demise to the back of my mind. A fae could get lost in the rolling emptiness of the ocean. I was determined to enjoy it while I could.

A svelte young man cut across my line of sight atop a skimboard as it sliced across the bubbling over-wash. His muscles flexed in an orchestra of perfectly timed twists and spins. A wave flipped his board in the air, and he caught it with one hand. His strawberry blond hair hung in wet tendrils down the tanned crevice between his shoulder blades.

The other skimboarders were good, but not that good. The young man practically glowed with the ionized magic of the shoreline. The beach was an in-between place, not quite land and not quite sea, yet a portal to both. It was unmistakable. He had Threshold Fae in him.

"Lil, you have that look on your face again."

"What look?" I asked, raising my eyebrows over my sunglasses in mock surprise.

"That's your work look." Dalia squinched her face into a tense mocking stare. It was a horrible impersonation.

"Okay, you're right." I leaned back in my beach chair and closed my eyes. "But that's not what I look like." She giggled and I joined in. Everyone needs a vacation once in a while.

THE END

What? You were expecting more? Oh, you want to know what happened to the Immortal Serpent and his nagas? I guess, being human, you're more concerned for the humans on the reservation. Look. I'll explain it again. I'm a chaos fae. Their problems are not my problems. I'm not the good guy. This was not a superhero story.

Those humans knew what they were doing. As for the Immortal Serpent, I won't tell anyone about his existence. He can do that himself if he's still there when the Council's collectors show up.

Don't look so shocked. If you make a deal with a fae, pay close attention to the verbiage. That's all the advice you'll get from me on the subject.

This is the end of the story. Thanks for being good little humans. You can exit through the giftshop. Bye.

~ Sneak Peek from Season Two ~

By the time I'd flown back from my lovely Florida vacation, things had gone critical in the Underhill. Something serious had happened inside our comfy, little underground pocket universe located just below downtown Baltimore. In general, Underhills were vast, cavernous entities of shifting rock and monolithic mood swings. Ours more so than others.

The Council had ordered an evacuation, but the thresholds going into and leading out of our ornery Locus Geographia had all closed. No one was talking about what had gone wrong. Hennig in Biomechanics and Gillian in Morphology were avoiding me, and my best friend, Daphne, wasn't returning my calls.

All work at the laboratory for Functional Anatomy and Evolution had ceased. Fae already outside of the Underhill were ordered to stay clear.

I couldn't go home. But I couldn't start looking for a job and a place of my own in the human world while in standby mode. That left me couch surfing with my human friends. Until I landed on the one couch I shouldn't have...Daniel's.

EXCERPT - DEVOURING THE DEMON

I stared at the human pregnancy test in utter disbelief. The Fae didn't have pregnancy tests, so I'd waited an entire month for my potential pregnancy hormones to match the levels of a human woman. And now the wait was over.

Knuckles rapped softly on the outside of the bathroom door.

"You okay in there?" Daniel's muffled voice softened with compassion.

He knew about my potential baby predicament, but he didn't know what that meant for me as a Lilith. My birthing curse wasn't exactly a topic for the dinner table. How does a girl work into conversation that she can't keep a child until she's killed one hundred of her previous offspring? It was a savagery only The Father Who Turned Away could remove from my kind.

Of all the different genetic phyla, classes, and families of fae the humans had learned of twenty years ago during the Revelation, Liliths were a genus humans just couldn't get enough of.

The Fae didn't have rock stars, or social media celebrities. We had demons and dragons, hags and trolls, and—yes—we had sex fairies. I was a walking, talking wet dream that absolutely no human could have sex with.

As a Lilith or, as the Talmud had labeled us—a Night Monster, my special genitals were designed to drain my lover's life force.

No, I still won't show you. Quit asking.

As it was, only the strongest of fae could knock boots with me, and that was iffy now that I'd consumed an unfathomable amount of mana. There was definitely no way Daniel and I could do the deed, no matter how badly we wanted to.

We'd spent three long weeks eating takeout, playing darts, and discussing everything but our feelings for each other.

He'd played the part of supportive friend, but our hugs were too long, our laughter too nervous, our glances too furtive.

Yes, I was attracted to that tall, tanned, bone-digger, but I liked his brain too. It helped that we were both paleontologists. Well, he was a paleontologist. I worked for a fae genetics lab connected to Hans Jodkins University's laboratory for Functional Anatomy and Evolution. We helped humans with their research and shared knowledge with them, but only the fae knew about our secretive breeding project.

The Council of Elders was hard at work rebuilding the fae population by recombining genes through forced copulation.

So, if you have even a drop of fae blood, you'd better keep it to yourself, or you'll be paired with a fae of your species and forced to fuck. Yep, old school. While we watch.

And, when I say our labs are connected, I mean our Underhill shares resources with the human lab through an aperture that spans our dimension and the human one. It's a fairly dangerous connection that can only be controlled by specialized threshold fae. Passing through it was a part of my daily routine. Or—it was—up until three weeks ago. Now, I can't get back into the Underhill to save my life.

"Yeah. I'm okay," I called through the closed door.

Though neither of us had voiced it, we'd both been hoping my test would be negative. We'd almost fooled ourselves into thinking there was a way a human and a Lilith could be intimate without the ensuing loss of life. Now that I'd received a giant upgrade in mana reserves, my eros was almost surely lethal to a human. And, on top of that...I was pregnant.

"I'm coming out." I flushed the toilet and took my time washing my trembling hands.

We'd discussed the differences in our life cycles as it pertained to dating. We'd faced the fact that I was much longer lived than he. Eventually, he'd grow old and die and, if we'd decided to be together, I'd potentially mourn him for centuries.

Boy, had the tables turned. Unless I killed the little life growing inside me at the moment of its birth, I'd be dead before I could hold it in my arms. In just a few months, I was going to suffer the same fate as my mother. She'd given her life so that I could live but, thanks to the curse, I'd never known her.

I know what you're thinking. No, there is nothing that can be done while the child is still inside me. Fae bodies protect their offspring above all else, and the curse is very specific.

"I know this is difficult and I hate to interrupt," Daniel's gentle voice strained, "but I think you have a message."

"A message?" I yanked the bathroom door open. The sudden whoosh of air blew his sun-bleached, cookie brown hair into his sulfuric aqua eyes.

He tucked the chin length strands behind his ear and nodded nervously.

"Where is it?" I looked at his empty hands.

"On the floor."

I searched the hardwood of the bedroom floor for a piece of paper. I checked the rug for an envelope. I found nothing.

Then, Daniel pointed to the fireplace, where the remains of last night's fire still glowed. A wisp of smoke dancing along the wood in front of the fireplace, and that's when I saw it. Several embers had jumped out of the grate and burned a message in his floor.

Lilith,

Bring the Swamp Witch.

Hurry!

-Hamus

Hamus! That judgmental, tyrannical prick! I had half a mind to pull up the floorboards flip them over, and ignore the draco-demon's message. If it had to do with Hamus, I wasn't interested. In fact, nothing about Hamus interested me…except maybe the way his fiery hair seemed to flicker brighter when I entered a room. Or the way his ruddy fire-light danced off his opalescent scales like rainbows. Or the way his molten chainmail skirt rode up sometimes, providing a quick glimpse of his best asset.

Hamus had a legendary cock which he had used to sire many lines of fae. But those days were gone. He hadn't taken a lover since his wife died nearly a century ago. He was strictly *look but don't touch*. Especially for me. Hamus hated Liliths and me in particular, though I had no idea why.

"Swamp Witch?" Daniel eyed the sooty message.

"I don't know a swamp witch."

"It sounds urgent."

It did, and since Hamus was a Council Member, I couldn't ignore his command.

My stomach turned.

I ran back to the bathroom.

Was it the pregnancy making me nauseous, or the thought of standing before that blood-thirsty council of ancient monsters? Or was it the idea of seeing Hamus again after our strange far-seeing encounter last month when I'd been trapped and on the verge of death. And he'd been…nice.

Who was the Swamp Witch? How could I find her? And why had Hamus reached out to *me*?

He loathed me.

He'd sooner kill me than work with me.

I'd missed something.

Something big.

ABOUT THE AUTHOR

For more tales of magic and dark desire, check out The Hell Gate Series published by The Wild Rose Press.

Facebook:
https://www.facebook.com/hunter.skye.12914/
Instagram:
https://www.instagram.com/hunterjskye/
Tiktok:
https://www.tiktok.com/@hunterskyebooks
Twitter:
https://twitter.com/hunterskyebooks
Goodreads:
https://www.goodreads.com/book/show/61421751
Website:
https://hunterskye.com/
Books:
https://linktr.ee/hunterjskye

Printed in the USA
CPSIA information can be obtained
at www.ICGtesting.com
CBHW021532270724
12257CB00023B/148